Ursula Hegi's
Floating in My Mother's Palm

"A graceful, lyrical, heartbreaking book that offers many pleasures, not the least of which is the opportunity to read a very talented author writing at the top of her form, telling stories she seems born to tell in a voice that is completely her own. Marvelous."
—Alice McDermott

"A treasure of a book. At once amazingly delicate and eerily powerful, it envelops the reader in the raw, painful, and poignant life of a small town in postwar Germany—benumbed, bewildered, and, sadly, not much the wiser. Ursula Hegi is a beautiful writer with much truth to tell."
—Lynne Sharon Schwartz

"Exquisite . . . Hegi's language signals a rare and particular power. There is a sonorous, hypnotic hum about these sentences that resound as prose, poetry, and hymn—and when we put the book down, its after-images burn the mind's eye."
—*San Francisco Review of Books*

"If Stravinsky were a writer, I imagine he would have written a book such as this, for Ursula Hegi gathers all the tonal moods and emotional power to her work that we expect of music that moves us to appreciate our hearts and souls and their troubling complexity."
—Bob Shacochis

Floating in My Mother's Palm

Other books by Ursula Hegi

Unearned Pleasures and Other Stories
Intrusions

Floating in My Mother's Palm

A Novel

Ursula Hegi

Vintage Contemporaries

VINTAGE BOOKS

A DIVISION OF RANDOM HOUSE, INC.

NEW YORK

FIRST VINTAGE CONTEMPORARIES EDITION, JUNE 1991

"Saving a Life" appeared in *American Fiction 88*, Wesley Press.
"Trudi Montag's Romantic Episode" won Honorable Mention in the
1988 New Letters Literary Award.

Library of Congress Cataloging-in-Publication Data
Hegi, Ursula.
Floating in my mother's palm: a novel/Ursula Hegi.—1st Vintage
contemporaries ed.
p.   cm.—(Vintage contemporaries)
ISBN 0-679-73115-6 (pbk.)
I. Title.
PR9110.9.H43F5 1991
823—dc20   90-50622
CIP

Manufactured in the United States of America
579B864

For my mother, Johanna

Acknowledgments

With deep gratitude to Susan Wheeler and Lesa Luders, who read early drafts of the manuscript and offered their insights and encouragement, and to Gordon, Eric, Adam, and my women's group, whose love and support have nurtured my writing.
I would also like to express my appreciation to the Washington State Arts Commission, Artist Trust, and the Northwest Institute for Advanced Study for grants which aided in the completion of this novel.

Floating in My Mother's Palm

✑ White Lilacs

W hen my mother entered her tenth month of carrying me, I stopped moving inside her womb. She awoke that morning to a sense of absolute silence that startled her out of dreams filled with flute music and colorful birds, dreams she'd never had until she became pregnant with me, dreams she would have again when, two years later, she carried my brother.

When I imagine my mother that morning, I see her lying alone in the double bed with the birch headboard. I have tried to imagine my father in the room with her, but I can't see him—only my mother who raises her nightgown and spreads both hands across her taut belly, waiting for me to move. On the window is a smudge where, just yesterday, she rested her forehead against the glass while gazing at the white lilac bush that grows behind the house. Nearly fourteen years later I will tear lilacs from that bush, wrap the stems in tissue paper, and carry them to the cemetery where I will drop them into my mother's open grave.

But this morning my mother's hands move across her abdomen as she tries to reassure herself of my life. All she feels is a cloak of fear that drapes itself around her. My mother waits. But her flesh does not stir against her palms. Sister Agathe will know, she thinks. She'll know what to do. The sister has taken care of my mother since the beginning of her pregnancy, answering her many questions with kindness.

When my mother leaves the house to walk to the hospital, Frau Talmeister, who used to be one year ahead of her in school, leans in the open living room window of the house across the street. Her elbows rest on pillows she has propped on the window sill. In one hand she holds a cup of coffee. Most of her days she spends like this, disappearing only for quick trips to the bathroom or to refill her cup.

Warm gusts of wind mold my mother's dress against her spine. She is a tall woman and carries me high. When I'm three she will tell me I slept under her heart, and I'll envision a warm and well-lit place where I waited to be born.

Her dress billows in front of her belly as she walks the five blocks to the Theresienheim, which contains the convent in one wing and the home for the aged in the other. A few of the rooms are kept available for childbirth and minor emergencies. Occasionally the nuns consult a doctor, but they prefer to deal with matters on their own. For surgery the people in Burgdorf travel the ten kilometers to one of the large hospitals in Düsseldorf.

Sister Agathe examines my mother. Warm and dry, her palms move across my mother's belly. She is a slight woman with patient eyes. Her strong hands have guided many infants from the womb. "The child needs rest too." She smiles at my mother. "It's normal."

My mother has trusted Sister Agathe ever since she was a girl and the sister removed a rusty nail from her bare foot. Twice her parents took her to the Theresienheim with a broken arm, and each time Sister Agathe set her bone without scolding her for being careless. When she became pregnant, my mother chose the sister instead of going to the midwife.

"It won't be long now." The sister's hand brushes a strand of damp hair from my mother's forehead.

My mother wants to believe her. Yet, she has felt my relentless movements for months now, growing more powerful with each day. To her, the cessation of my efforts signals something terribly wrong.

"Go home now," the sister tells her. "Rest if you can."

It has taken my mother four years of marriage to become pregnant. "But what if something is wrong?"

"Nothing is wrong. I wish you wouldn't worry."

Though my mother wants to protest, she sits up and lowers her dress. Her steps echo through the tiled halls of the convent. Outside, the spring air is tinged with scents of cinnamon and vanilla. At the corner the Hansen bakery truck stands parked, its side panel open to display loaves of crisp bread, glazed buns, and pastries.

Three days of waiting press my mother into cold swells of fear that she tries to ease with prayers she can't finish because she keeps forgetting words, entire lines.

"Move," she whispers to me while my father sleeps next to her.

"Move," she screams at me when she is alone.

Her hands keep returning to her belly, which is low and massive and still. She tries to paint, but the shapes don't match her vision, and the colors feel flat. She builds an oak frame for a painting she finished last February of deer grazing among blue winter trees. Bare patches show through the snow-covered ground where the deer search for grass. Their bellies are white reflections of the snow.

When finally she feels the tightening of her uterus—like monthly cramps, only stronger—she envisions the child within her stirring again. But this feels different, not the shape of a head or limb expanding her abdomen for an instant, but rather an ultimate rising of her center toward something unknown, yet familiar.

It is early, a quarter past six, when she walks back to the convent. Frau Talmeister's window is closed. The streets are vacant. A few of the buildings are still piles of rubble from the war that ended last year, but most of the houses have been rebuilt. The leaves of the chestnut trees cast long shadows across the sidewalk. My mother walks along Schreberstrasse, past the brook where, as a girl, she used to swing herself across the shallow water, gripping the branches of the willow that grows high and wide above the brook. She passes the playground where empty benches surround the sandbox. Without motion the swings hang from their steel frames.

The Theresienheim is locked. Beams of sun break the chill of morning and strike the stained-glass windows of the chapel, fanning into feathers of blood and sky. My mother rings the bell outside the carved door. Her legs feel cold and heavy. She hesitates before she rings again.

After what seems like a long time, a young postulant opens the door far enough to block it with her body. "The sisters are in church."

"I need to see Sister Agathe. The child—"

"Can you come back in an hour?"

"—it's about to be born, I think."

The postulant averts her eyes from my mother's belly as if ashamed for her. "The sisters need their breakfast after mass."

"Sister Agathe would want to know." Pain presses itself through my mother's womb, enshrouds her spine—white wafers of fire.

"I'm not allowed to call them out of church." The postulant falters. "But I'll let you wait," she whispers and opens the door further to let my mother in. "Over there."

She points to the bench under the painting of Jesus exposing his bleeding heart through the blue folds of his tunic.

My mother gathers her hands across her huge belly, as if holding me like this will somehow protect both of us. Carefully, she lowers herself onto the rigid bench. The high voices of the nuns glide through the closed door of the chapel, weightless above the current of the organist's "Ave Maria," a river of sound that spills across my mother and makes her wish she could drift within it. But she is seized by another contraction, and despite her bulk, she feels incredibly small, much smaller than the cry that escapes her.

When the nuns file out of the chapel, their black habits swish in soft waves around their shoes. Heads bent, hands tucked into the opposite ends of their sleeves, they walk silently past my mother, whose hands grip the plank of the bench. Her face feels numb from trying to hold the pain within herself.

"Here. Let me." Sister Agathe separates herself from the line of nuns. Gently, she grasps my mother's elbow and leads her down a long corridor, past open doors that frame the beds of the old people who live here. In an empty white room, she helps my mother climb on a long table covered with a starched sheet. "I'm sorry you had to wait for me." Running her hands across my mother's belly, she stands with her head tilted as if listening for the sound of something far away.

"Can you feel—"

"Wait." Her palms prod my mother's sides as though trying to lift the child through the wall of flesh.

Suddenly my mother finds it difficult to breathe. "Sister Agathe—"

"Wait," the sister says again. "Please?" A fine layer of sweat has formed above her upper lip. "I'll be back in a minute." Without looking at my mother, she leaves the room.

My mother guides her hands along the familar outline of

her belly which is taut and still. She draws in a deep breath that makes the skin beneath her fingers expand. Carefully she releases it, then draws in another long breath and holds it.

When Sister Agathe returns, she brings Sister Ingeborg, the supervisor of nurses; she tells my mother to move her palms from her abdomen and replaces them with her own pale hands.

Into the silence my mother blurts, "You must call a doctor. Please!" It takes courage for her to request this. She has grown up in this town. Has grown up with these sisters who teach school and tend to the ill. With these sisters who've become accustomed to the obedience they've nurtured in women and children.

The sisters glance at each other as Sister Agathe steps back from the table. She pulls a handkerchief from her sleeve, dabs at her upper lip.

"The child—" Sister Ingeborg shakes her head. "It's too late. You've carried the child too long."

My mother feels her womb tighten in protest under the nun's touch. She raises herself on her elbows, searches Sister Agathe's face for some signal, some promise, but the sister's eyes flicker away, and her fingers stray to the rosary hanging from her belt.

"The child's soul is with the Lord now." Sister Ingeborg's voice is calm. Assuring. "Your body will expel it whenever it is ready."

During my first year of life, when she nurses me, my mother will often recall the rage that sprang up within her at the nun's words, a rage that gave her the courage to hoist herself from the white table and walk from the room, from the hospital and into the street where the Hansen bakery truck was parked. She persuaded the driver, Herr Meier, to close the side panel and drive her to the midwife's house. Inside the white truck with the blue lettering, surrounded by the fresh dough smell of the morning loaves, she felt her contractions become a pulse independent of her own, swallowing her own, a red pulse of rage that sustained the only faith she was capable of—that the child within her was alive.

Trudi Montag's Romantic Episode

I don't know how often our housekeeper told me the story of Trudi Montag's fall—perhaps only once. All I remember is that I grew up with her story and imagined her many times as an infant falling from her mother's arms. Each time I pictured the fall in slow motion, Trudi landed on her head with a soft, sick plop—never on the side or the back of her head, always the top. And then she rolled over and lay still. Very still.

The accident, I believed, stunted her growth and destroyed her mother's sanity. She refused to touch the child at all and took to hiding behind St. Martin's Church, pressing herself against the arched door of the sacristy with her arms flung out as if waiting for someone to drive nails through her palms and into the oiled wood. The pastor would call her husband, who'd pry her off the door and carry her home. But he couldn't stay with her every moment, and soon she'd be back at the sacristy door, taller than the priest and certainly more impassioned, barring his entrance to the sacred chalices and vestments. After she was sent off to the Grafenberg asylum, Trudi was raised by her father who ran the pay-library, where, for a few pfennige, the people in Burgdorf could borrow romances, American westerns, nurse-and-doctor novels, mysteries, and war novels—books that the church library refused to have on its shelves.

Between the stacks of books the child played with dolls whose heads were well-shaped and in the right proportion to the rest of their bodies. Customers occasionally picked her up and stroked her silver-blond hair, telling her what pretty curls she had, while over her shoulder they whispered to her father, "The poor little thing."

By the time I was twelve, Trudi Montag had inherited the pay-library. Though she was in her early forties, she was less than one meter twenty tall. Her shoulders were broad, her head too large. I have pictured her as a girl, growing until she was ten or eleven. Perhaps something at the top of her head had closed her off where her mother had dropped her, while inside her body the growing continued. Where could it go except spread outward? Into her face, her shoulders, her hips. Sideways. Into her legs, her fingers, stretching her skin until it was tight.

She knew everything. As soon as it happened. Before it happened. She had the dubious gift of guessing what went on behind closed doors. These insights she embroidered into stories which she circulated around town. Bearer of news—good and bad—she walked through the streets of Burgdorf on O-shaped legs, wearing cardigans that never quite closed over the wide bosom of her striped housedresses, moving with the assurance one usually sees in women who are truly beautiful. To each encounter she brought her friendly curiosity; yet, when people saw her advancing toward them, they expected the worst; even good news barely made up for that first sense of dread they'd felt at the sight of her.

On the surface Burgdorf was a town of great virtues

while underneath all kinds of transgressions were hushed up. It was a town of pretend where many adults, after tremendous failings, would fabricate proper lives, and the town would pretend along with them, protecting that shallow veneer of respectability. Herr Pastor Beier, who listened to the confessions of countless sins, could be counted on to whitewash them all through absolution, but Trudi Montag would not let the town forget any of its flaws.

Every day at noon, as soon as the bells from St. Martin's rang, she closed her library for two hours, ate a slab of black bread with Dutch cheese and sliced tomatoes, and set out to carry the morning's gossip through town. Taking up most of the sidewalk, she took strategic sweeps past those places that enriched and distributed her supply of information: Becker's grocery store, the midwife's house, Frau Talmeister's window, Anton Immers's butcher shop, the Hansen bakery truck. . . . Like an ancient trader, she bartered until she had extracted a piece of new gossip from her listeners.

Our housekeeper, Frau Brocker, was one of Trudi's reluctant messengers; she liked to pretend she'd known about something all along. It irritated her to be fed a generous amount of local news; yet, she would have complained had Trudi Montag excluded her. My mother, who considered gossip cheap, said it was the one side of Frau Brocker she didn't like.

In her pay-library Trudi Montag told me that my mother had stopped going to church after my brother, Joachim, had died, that our housekeeper's son, Rolf, was illegitimate, and that my great-uncle Alexander had leapt from the attic window of the four-story house he had built, the house that my mother had inherited and where we still lived in a large apartment on the first floor. As a young man Alexander had lost his wife to tuberculosis, and he'd never remarried or had children. Though Trudi Montag hadn't actually witnessed his fall, she'd seen the spot on the side- walk where he'd landed, and she'd talked with Frau Tal- meister who'd seen it happen from her window across the street.

"He wore his best suit," Trudi Montag said, "and a white carnation in his lapel. He opened his arms as if to fly." Her words painted him for me, the unsmiling man I'd seen only in faded sepia photos, his sandy hair cut close to his skull, standing rigidly in formal clothes as he stared into the camera. *He climbs out of the attic window. Stands on the flat section of tiles four stories above the street. The air feels cool against his face, and he smoothes his Kaiser Wilhelm mustache. Spreading his arms in the prelude to an embrace, he leaps out of those posed photographs.*

"We would have told you eventually," my father said when I asked him about my great-uncle's suicide. "Once you're older. It happened long before you were born. Trudi Montag had no business telling you. I wish you'd stay away from her and those trashy books."

In front of the pay-library stood an old chestnut tree that carried huge blossom candles in the spring. I'd flatten my- self against its trunk, scanning the street to make sure my father wouldn't see me before I entered. The kitchen be- hind the library led into a living room with a huge gold fish tank and a blue velvet sofa. If I sat next to Trudi Montag on the sofa, I'd find myself sliding toward her along the slope created by her weight. Instead of pictures, she had mirrors on her living room walls, small mirrors of all shapes in ornate frames.

When I was her only customer, she sometimes brewed rosehip tea, and we'd sip the hot, sweet liquid. I'd lean my head against the velvet and listen to her stories about her Aunt Helene who'd left town to move to America and marry a man whose first two wives had died in childbirth, about the Romans who'd marched through Burgdorf nearly 2000 years ago, about old Anton Immers who sacrificed his violet plants to ensure survival of the fittest, about the midwife who—twelve years ago—had suddenly appeared with an infant though no one had seen her pregnant, about Napoleon who had stayed in our town, about Frau Buttgereit's kidney stones which were the size of robins' eggs, about the knights who once lived in the Sternburg, a small castle with a baroque tower near the chapel.

My mother had painted the Sternburg many times. It used to be a fortress with a drawbridge, but hundreds of years ago it was turned into a farm with wheat fields and meadows where white cows grazed in the sun. The moat was still there, filled with scummy water. Bright green moss had eaten into the trunks of the poplars that bordered the dirt road around the moat. It was a good place to catch green and yellow caterpillars.

Sometimes Trudi Montag brought out her antique collection of cut-out dolls that were made of glossy cardboard, and we pinched costumes onto the paper dolls by bending tabs around their hips or shoulders. They had elaborate hats and ball gowns and old-fashioned bathing suits. Within seconds we could change a doll's appearance as the paper body disappeared behind a layer of colorful clothes that looked out of style and romantic.

"I had my romantic episode," Trudi told me one afternoon as she fastened a pink ball gown to the shoulders of a blond paper doll. "Fifteen years ago. He was a little older than I, with black hair and a mustache. I met him on the jetty near the Braunmeiers' farm. It was a summer evening, still light." She gazed past me, a soft expression on her round face as if she saw herself on the jetty, wearing the linen dress that made her look taller. "I could have married," she said, and I didn't dare ask her why she hadn't, because I'd heard a different story from Frau Brocker. According to her, Trudi Montag could have gotten herself raped or killed. But not married.

She used to walk to the Rhein some evenings and sit by the water, watching the current go by, waiting for something she couldn't define. She'd watch the swallows flit across the water like mosquitoes, almost touching the surface before rising again, and wish she were as lithe as they.

If she wasn't home by nine, her father would drive out to the Braunmeier's farm, climb the dike, and shout her name. But that evening her father was late. The opposite bank of the Rhein was already shrouded in dusk. Trees and shrubs were taking on shapes that looked denser than during the day; freighters moved slowly like spirits lulled by fog. Only a short while ago she'd been able to make out their names—*Brabo 4, Antwerpen, Birseck, Antigone, Mannheim, Valleria*—but now the fading light only gave her their profiles, some of their hulls low in the water, others without cargo.

A three-quarter moon moved out from behind a cloud, and it looked as if the main part of the river flowed north while, near the embankment, it seemed to work its way south. Where the two currents merged, a silver line shimmered under the moon, shifted, and adjusted itself, over and over.

"What are you doing here?" A tall man dropped his bicycle against the rocks and walked out to her as if they'd agreed to meet there. His face was lean, his skin tanned. He wore his dark hair longer than the men in town. Without waiting for her answer, he asked, "Can you swim here?"

She nodded, staying seated and straightening her spine so she'd look taller. As he sat down on a rock across from her, she was certain he was the most appealing man she'd ever seen, and it suddenly came to her that it was he she'd been waiting for all those times she had come to the river alone, driven by a familiar longing that hadn't made sense to her.

"Do you swim?" he asked.

"Sometimes."

"Is it dangerous?"

"Not if you stay close to shore." She wanted to ask where he came from, where he would go after he left her.

"Will you swim with me?" His voice was soft.

"I don't have a swimsuit."

"Neither do I. Would anyone mind?"

"No one is here."

He smiled at her. "You are."

She glanced down at the skirt that hid her wide thighs and hips. A gentle breeze rose from the river and lifted her pale hair from her shoulders, cooling the back of her neck. Along the sides of the jetty the river touched the rocks in calm bands while, at the tip, the water was restless, as if it were boiling, moving in countless directions at once.

"I like your hair," he said. "And your voice though you haven't said much."

"Not yet."

He nodded as though he were promising her many long talks and looked into her eyes until, for the first time in her life, she felt beautiful. She saw herself dancing with him on the white excursion boat that floated on the Rhein every Friday and Saturday night during the summer, with lanterns strung along its sides, music tinting the banks along the way any color you wanted. She'd heard that music many times, and it had followed her into her dreams, the color of fuchsias.

"Will you swim with me?" he asked again.

She smiled, knowing he had meant to ask, *Will you dance with me?* "Soon," she said. "Soon."

The man raised one hand and, like a sleepwalker wiping aside the remnants of a dream, pulled the suspenders away from his shoulders. "Will you watch my clothes and bike for me?"

"Yes," she said, feeling light and tall and limber.

His chest was tanned and smooth. She didn't look away when he took off his belt but acted as if she'd seen naked men before, and kept looking at him until, from a distance, she heard her father calling her name.

"Don't," she whispered as the man flew into his clothes and leapt on his bike. "Don't—"

"She was there, on the jetty, in plain view with a naked man," our housekeeper told me. We sat at our kitchen table, eating thick slices of her warm peach pie with whipped cream.

"She was only watching his clothes for him."

"You really believe that, Hanna?"

I nodded.

"If her father hadn't come in time to chase him off—"

"He wasn't like that, the man," I said quickly. "He—"

She laughed. Squinted at me. "And what kind of man would you say he was?"

"Someone who—who saw her . . . and that she was special."

"I think—" She stopped as my mother's steps approached.

My mother's hands were smudged with paint. She wore one of my father's old shirts which she kept in her studio upstairs. The smoke from her cigarette coiled itself around her wrist. "Trudi's father," she said, giving Frau Brocker an amused look, "would have done a much wiser thing if he'd let his daughter make her own choices that evening."

But Frau Brocker shook her head as she cut a piece of pie for my mother. "God knows what would have happened to her then," she said.

. . .

Nothing much did happen to Trudi Montag, at least not in the conventional sense of things that happened to women of her generation in our town. No wedding in St. Martin's Church. No husband to come home to her every evening. No children to cling to her hands for a few brief years. Yet, she'd had her romantic episode by the river and the courage to cherish that encounter and let it nurture her through the years while, within her, the stories of other people's lives ripened and took shape.

One summer, when I returned to Burgdorf as an adult, I found a glistening red pebble by the river in the crevice between two wet rocks. In my hand it dried and turned brown, ordinary. Yet, I knew the promise to shine had been there all along. Rubbing my thumb across its drab surface, I thought of Trudi Montag: I remembered sitting next to her on the blue velvet sofa, remembered the sweet taste of rose-hip tea, remembered a morning, not too long ago, when I'd bent to lift my son from his crib and—all at once—had been caught by a sense of dread as I saw Trudi Montag falling, falling from her mother's arms in slow motion. For a moment I'd stood frozen before I'd dared to gather my son in my arms, although, by then, I knew that Trudi Montag's deformity had nothing to do with a fall. She was a dwarf whose size had been used as a warning for many children: *If you eat butter with a spoon you'll look like Trudi Montag when you grow up. . . . If you don't wash your knees . . . If you don't finish your red cabbage . . . If you pick up this baby it might end up just like Trudi Montag. . . .* Fragments of warnings, they had come together to form the essence of one woman.

I sat down on a rock and linked my arms around my knees. Across the Rhein, clumps of sheep grazed in a meadow, circled by a long-haired dog. The current flowed north, but a southern wind stirred across its surface, and as the sun caught the ripples here and there like lights dancing in a mirror, I saw Trudi Montag moving through her rooms—a short, heavy woman with white hair—seeking her reflection in the many small mirrors that covered her walls, mirrors in golden frames, none of them large enough to embrace all of her at once.

Oma

After my Oma's right leg was amputated, she was fitted with a wooden leg which she wore when she left the building; inside her apartment she got around by resting her knee stump on a chair and sliding the chair across the floor. She was my father's mother and had grown up in a family where good manners and proper clothes were esteemed above everything else. Early on she had rejected those values when she decided to study music and philosophy, wearing out-of-date clothing so she could afford books. She had more books than anyone I knew—leather-bound collections of poetry, thick volumes of philosophy, large books with prints of famous paintings, stacks of yellowed journals from her years of teaching philosophy at the university. Her hair, which had been red like my father's when she was younger, had turned white and she wore it in a braid around her head.

One evening, while my father watched her make her awkward way from her kitchen to the living room, it came to him how much easier it would be for her if the chair were closer to the ground. He sawed two centimeters off the chair's legs, wrapped the ends in layers of green felt, and fastened the material with electrical tape. It not only made it easier for Oma to slide the chair across the floor, it also eliminated the familiar scratching of wood against linoleum. She'd appear almost soundlessly, startling us who had grown accustomed to hearing the chair legs announce her arrival.

Though my parents had urged her several times to move in with us, she insisted on living alone in her Düsseldorf apartment. Many Saturday afternoons I visited her, and we'd listen to music that swelled through the rooms and roused feelings within me so powerful I couldn't name them; yet, the best of our moments together were tinged with my sadness that, soon, I'd have to leave her again.

Two years after the amputation Oma felt a tingling in her good leg below the knee, a sensation that grew into a burning pain and woke her from nights of troubled sleep. The pain spread into her toes. Sores and blisters bred on her foot. And when the pain subsided, a numbness set in that made her leg turn cold and white. With her right leg my Oma had welcomed that numbness until it was too late to save it; but this time she knew it could mean the loss of her left leg and asked my parents to take her to St. Lukas Hospital.

Her doctor prescribed antibiotics and confined Oma to a narrow white room on the second floor with a view of the *Hofgarten*. But she was too ill to look out the window and watch the swans and ducks in the pond or the children who rode their bicycles along the tree lined paths of the park. Some mornings, when my mother visited her, Oma lay covered with five blankets; yet, her body shivered. My father arrived in the late afternoons after treating his last dental patient and sat on the edge of her bed.

One rainy October day, when he closed his practice early to be with his mother, he laid one hand against her pale face. Her white hair had thinned so much that her scalp was beginning to show. Her fingers trembled on the layers of blankets. All his life he'd seen her strong, taking care of him and his two sisters after his father had died young from a burst appendix. Eyes burning, he bent to kiss her dry cheek. She looked away from him as if ashamed of her weakness.

Outside the window, trees stood gray and stark against the sky as they had that Thursday in 1941, nearly seventeen years before, when one of Oma's students had called my father to tell him she'd been arrested during her philosophy class. She'd been warned twice but had refused to adapt her lectures to Third Reich views. Four months later, when she returned from the prison camp where she was held with other German intellectuals whose ideas were considered treacherous, she was forced to resign from the university.

When my father left Oma's room, her doctor walked toward him in the corridor. The skin around his eyes was unlined, but where his face thickened around the jaw, it had settled into deep creases. "She's putting up a good fight, your mother."

"Do you see any improvement?"

"Some." The doctor's eyes were gray. Watery. "Still— we need to think about last rites."

"No," my father said. "No.

"She's ill. Very ill."

"It would frighten her."

The doctor shook his head. "Even if we decide to amputate—I doubt she'll leave here alive."

My father turned from him and walked back into his mother's room. Swiftly he gathered the blankets around her and lifted her from the bed.

"What are you doing?" The doctor tried to block his way.

"She is leaving here alive."

"You can't—"

"If she has to die, it will happen at home." Through the layers of blankets my father felt his mother's fever. Her flushed face sank against his shoulder as he carried her past the doctor.

In the week after my father brought Oma to our apartment, she grew stronger with each day as the fever released her body. While my mother painted upstairs in her studio, Oma and I looked through the books she'd asked my father to get from the shelves in her living room, books with magnificent photos of old paintings, and she'd tell me stories about the women and men who'd painted them.

My grandmother must have first noticed the smell in the healer's apartment—a blend of camomile tea and worn socks that she'd describe to me later, a smell that threaded itself through the hallway and into the living room where the old man had taken her and my parents. The skin on his bald head looked as if it had been made for the skull of someone larger, heavier; yet, his eyes were brown and clear —the eyes of a much younger man. While he led my father into the kitchen for a cup of tea, my mother undressed Oma in the living room.

She took off the silk dress and slip.

She unhooked the salmon-colored corset with the stays.

She unlaced my Oma's left shoe, then exposed her right leg where the shiny layer of skin at the end of the knee stump was drawn together in one puckered knot like an inside-out stocking pulled over a darning egg.

Despite the doubts that had almost kept her from coming to the healer's apartment, Oma let my mother help her climb on the padded table and cover her with a frayed, clean sheet. When my mother called for the old man, he sent her to wait with my father in the kitchen.

Raised on her elbows, my grandmother watched the healer. From a bottle he shook a few drops of oil into his hands. It smelled of almonds. Inside the bottle floated the pit of a peach or something that looked very much like it. He rubbed the oil into his palms, and when he began massaging my Oma's foot, his hands felt warm against her skin as if the oil had been heated. His fingers were blunt, his nails cut short.

He closed his eyes as he laid both hands on my Oma's left knee. "Oh yes," he said. "I thought so. . . . There's a lot here, a lot of things you've carried with you, that you're holding on to. Your body—you've been pushing too hard, wanting to do it all alone." His hand cupping her heel, he tried to push her toes back with his other hand. "So stiff," he murmured. "So stiff. Not yielding like the foot of a woman."

At first my Oma must have been embarrassed to have this stranger touch her foot, which has hardened with age. But his hands were soothing, and she sank deeper into the padded table. He asked her to lie on her stomach and gave her a folded towel to rest her head upon. One cheek against the mended terry cloth, she lay on the table, oddly at ease as the healer shook warm drops of oil on her back and kneaded them gently into her skin. Since my grandfather's death, no man had seen my Oma undressed. Pleasure from touch had only come from her own hands, but now she felt herself stretching, widening under the hands of the healer, hands that rose from her back like the pearl gray wings of a dove, then lowered themselves like feathers brushing her skin.

Suddenly one of his fingers grazed her spine between her shoulders, and it felt as if a knife were pressing into her. She roared up.

"That's part of it," he whispered. "A lot of things have become part of your body, things we need to dissolve."

She made herself sink back down, her face on the towel. His finger traced the outline of her spine like a white-hot blade—light, piercing.

"Are you using something? It feels like—"

"Only my hands," he said, moving them in front of her where she could see them, the nails so short that the fleshy tip of each finger protruded. "Do you want me to go on?"

Though she remembered the pain, she could not recall its intensity as she looked at his broad hands. She closed her eyes, nodded, and willed herself to absorb the healing, to believe in it, to dissolve whatever stood in its way. When she had first heard about the healer from one of her old students, she couldn't imagine anything beyond a laying on of hands the way Jesus did with the lepers, but this felt as if he were slicing through layers of muscles, shifting things dormant inside her.

I'm healing, she promised herself, trying not to flinch from him. That evening, when she returned to our apartment where she would stay with us through the rest of October and most of November, she undressed and checked her body for marks in front of the closet mirror, expecting to find red scratches, if not gashes, covering her back. Yet her skin would be unscathed, certain proof of his powers. Something within her already knew this, though she would have to test it later. And so she lay silent, my grandmother, face pressed into the towel to muffle involuntary screams, fingers gripping the edges of the padded table on either side of her head.

Each time the healer lifted his hands from her, she felt no pain at all. Her skin didn't even tingle. It was hot in the room, hot and still. When the healer asked her to turn around, she followed his voice, somehow not minding that all she wore were white cotton underpants—not that new —and that her pale breasts flattened themselves against her ribs.

The healer rubbed almond-smelling oil on her belly; his

right hand glided across her skin and opened up a warmth low within her. Only his index finger touched her—no harder than she would touch a child's face to remove a loose eyelash—yet, she felt the searing tip of a blade though the pain was lessened by an odd sense of peace, as if she'd been inside this room with the old man for days, or forever— she couldn't tell which—and he knew everything there was to know about her.

Months later, after her leg had healed, after the pain had contained itself into smaller and smaller areas until it had stopped entirely, after the sores and blisters had closed over with new, pink skin, my Oma recalled the sudden urgency that made her want to ask the old man how he worked his healing, and she was glad she'd remained silent because, even then, she sensed what she now believed—that only the gift can be shared, not the secret.

Maikäfer flieg
Dein Vater is im Krieg
Deine Mutter ist im Pommerland
Pommerland is abgebrannt
Maikäfer flieg

Ladybug fly
Your father is in the war
Your mother is in Pommerland
Pommerland has burned away
Ladybug fly
                    (German nursery rhyme)

✐ Women in Distress

When our housekeeper, Klara Brocker, was alone in our apartment, she read romances that she borrowed from Trudi Montag's pay-library. Except for names and settings the novels were alike and invariably ended with promises of eternal love and weddings. Perhaps Frau Brocker had heard those promises of eternal love too, but there'd been no wedding. The American soldier she'd met at the end of the war had left Burgdorf long before her son, Rolf, was born.

Frau Brocker hid the romances under the cover of our ironing board from where I retrieved them late at night and, with a flashlight under my blanket, read about women in distress and the men who rescued them. Each book jacket showed a beautiful woman leaning against something while she looked up at a man who wasn't leaning against anything. My mother never leaned or slouched.

I was careful not to move the folded tissue Frau Brocker kept inserted as a bookmark, and if she ever suspected I read her romances, she didn't say. A faster reader than she, I'd finish the novels days ahead of her and feel disappointed when, during one of my late night raids, I'd still find the same book. By the time I was twelve, I'd gone through everything we had on the birch shelves in our living room —the leather-bound volumes of Tolstoi my mother had given my father one Christmas, biographies of opera singers and painters, novels by Sigrid Undset and Thomas Mann—and I'd become as involved with Maria Callas and Anna Karenina as with the leaning women in Frau Brocker's books.

Klara Brocker did not look like the women on the book jackets, though she wore bright lipstick and plucked her eyebrows into thin arches; instead of flowing gowns and high-heeled sandals she wore cotton shifts and white sneakers. Every three months she got a new permanent that drew her brown hair close against her scalp in spiral curls. Sometimes I wondered if she was waiting for a man to rescue her from the life that was so different from the lives of the women in the romances: she lived with her son, Rolf, and her mother, who'd had a stroke and was paralyzed on one side of her body.

Every day at one, when I came home from school, my mother left her studio and my father closed his dental office for an hour. Before we sat down to eat the meal Frau Brocker had prepared for us, she wrapped half of the food in towels to keep it hot and carried it in a basket to her apartment where she ate with her mother and Rolf.

Though she earned enough to rent a better place, she lived on the fourth floor of Barbarossastrasse 15, an old building with a dark staircase. She had three rooms: the narrow bedroom that she shared with her mother, a kitchen, and the living room where Rolf slept on the sofa.

She gave most of her money to St. Martin's Church and tried to teach Rolf and me that only sacrifices brought real rewards. Those lessons were usually urged upon us when we sat at our kitchen table, eating thick pieces of her fruit pies or marbled pound cake. Our mouths full, we'd glance at each other, then at her, and nod.

The one indulgence she allowed herself was Gauloises, French cigarettes in a blue pack with the picture of a winged helmet, but even those she rationed, smoking only five a day. Unlike my mother who smoked while she did other things, Frau Brocker would stop whatever she was doing before she opened the silver foil at the top of the blue pack and lit one of the cigarettes.

On Sundays she wore tailored dresses that showed off her narrow waist and patent-leather shoes with medium-high heels. During mass she knelt in the third pew on the right side. Above the altar were three stained-glass windows; red, white, and black, they formed a pattern of hundreds of small crosses that intersected and overlapped. Frau Brocker was one of many people in Burgdorf who didn't like the modern design. The original windows, shattered by bombs, had been replaced after the war. She preferred the old windows along the sides of the church; their blues and purples and golds formed stars that softened the incoming light. But the light above the altar was harsh as though the solitary priest on the marble stairs, raising the sacred chalice in an ancient ceremony, had little to do with her.

Saturday afternoons she parted the purple drapes of the confessional and confessed her sins to Herr Pastor Beier who sat behind the latticed wall, one ear tilted toward her sins. Long ago he must have granted her absolution for her biggest transgression, because she continued to raise her face toward the communion and to bring the consequence of her sin—Rolf—to church with her.

Every March and September the potato man, Herr Weinhart, refilled the wooden bin in Klara Brocker's cellar.

New potatoes would tumble from his burlap sack through the open top of the bin, covering old layers of tired potatoes whose wrinkled skins had been pierced by pale sprouts. She would look forward to eating the new potatoes, their firm flesh coated with butter. But she'd have to use up the old ones first, peel the gray skin from their flaccid centers, and submerge them in boiling water. By the time the new potatoes dropped to the trapdoor in front of the bin, they too would look wrinkled and gray. To buy smaller quantities would have been more expensive, and so she ordered fifty kilos twice a year.

That March, when the potato man rang the bell, she met him by the front door, the cellar key in her hand. He was a tall man with a wide smile. The burlap sack slung over one shoulder, he walked down the basement stairs ahead of her. Blond, curly hair covered his arms and wrists where the sleeves of his blue shirt had slipped up.

She shared the cellar with five other tenants; each of them had one section. In the dim light she found the keyhole while Herr Weinhart waited next to her. He smelled of new, clean sweat. Gray light, filtered through cobwebs and coal dust, kept the cellar just short of total darkness and deepened the corner shadows. She'd hidden here with her mother during air raids, safe—it turned out—while other buildings in town had been hit by bombs that made them look like broken teeth with blackened edges.

Her hand reached for the chain that hung from the ceiling bulb, and she stepped aside to let Herr Weinhart walk past. He stood before the rising clouds of dust as the potatoes rumbled into the open bin, then he shook the corners of the sack, and folded the burlap into a square. Though he didn't resemble the American, his movements were the same, the long limbs and broad span of his shoulders.

"I guess that's all," he said and turned to leave.

She wanted to touch his cheek lightly, to run one finger along his throat.

"Are you coming up too?"

She crossed her arms. "In a while. You go ahead." Her face hot, she listened to the sound of his footsteps moving away from her on the cellar stairs. The peculiar, dark odor of mold, cobwebs and dampness pressed against her. She pushed back her shoulders, shook her head.

The walls were lined with shelves, heavy with jars that sealed within them the flavor and smell of fruits and vegetables she'd canned last summer. On the third shelf stood jars with hazy contents, left over from her mother: APPLE-SAUCE 1948, BEANS 1950, STRAWBERRY MARMALADE 1949. Behind them stood two dusty bottles, the years 1924 and 1923 barely legible on the faded labels. They bore a different handwriting, the Old German script of her grandmother, who died before Klara was born.

Whenever she thought of throwing these bottles out, she felt an odd sense of resistance, as if they connected her to a simpler past. She held one of them against the light. The liquid was cloudy, thick. Hard to imagine the ripe cherries or strawberries whose juices had been squeezed into the neck of this bottle. The cork was crumbling and musty. It had smelled like that during the war. "I should throw these bottles out," her mother had said more than once. "They're probably pure poison by now." But she'd only moved them further back to make room for the blankets she kept in the cellar for air raids.

Cautiously Klara returned the bottle to the shelf. None of the jars bore dates between 1942 and 1945. Anyone lucky enough to have food had eaten it. Except for the eighteen jars of peaches she and her mother had canned. A week after the American had been stationed in their building, he'd carried a crate of peaches up four flights of stairs to their apartment. He set the crate on their kitchen table and, while she and her mother watched, pried open the top to reveal golden-pink peaches, layers and layers of them. Her mouth suddenly dry, she ran her fingers across their fuzzy skins.

He laughed. "Here. Eat." He held one of the peaches out to her. His teeth were white, and his short hair exposed a small, leaf-shaped birthmark on his forehead. On his left hand he wore a ring.

When Klara bit into the peach, juice dribbled down her chin, and she wiped it with the back of her left hand. At first she chewed slowly, embarrassed that he was watching her, but as the hunger rose from her belly to meet the food, she assuaged it by taking another bite. She couldn't remember ever tasting anything so sweet, so good, and after the American left, she and her mother stood next to the table, eating peaches until their stomachs felt taut and the fronts of their dresses were damp with juice. Even after they gave some of the peaches to Herr Flemern, the tailor who lived on the first floor, and ate all the peaches they desired for an entire week, they had enough left to fill eighteen glass jars which they saved on the windowsill in the kitchen for special occasions. Amber half suns, the peaches floated in their own juice, emitting a golden glow that warmed the apartment.

Most of the peaches were still there when the American left three months later, but Klara wasn't able to swallow them. Though her mother ate some, the remaining jars sat on the windowsill until Rolf was old enough to take solid food and eat them mashed, his one legacy from his father.

The relentless hunger of those years—occasionally Klara still felt it, even after a large meal. She felt it now as she looked at the shabby leather suitcase next to the cellar door. During the war it used to stand behind the sofa in the living room, packed with clothing and food. That was before the American had arrived. Whenever the sirens sounded off, she'd grab the suitcase with one hand, her mother's arm with the other, and they'd rush down the stairs into the cellar, often without slippers, just wearing their nightgowns, and sit on layers of blankets that couldn't block the chill of the cement floor. Though she was in her late teens and taller than her mother, Klara let herself be folded into her mother's arms.

Eyes wide open in the dark, she thought of her father, who was fighting on the Russian front. His regiment had a goat, and when he sent photos, they'd be of him and several other men in uniforms, one of them always sitting on the goat. It seemed like a different war, not the kind where you hid from bombs, but where you could sit on a goat and laugh into a camera.

Sometimes she faded into sleep, rocking in her mother's arms, and whenever she woke up, her mother smiled although the corners of her mouth trembled. "Don't be afraid," she'd whisper.

Klara wasn't afraid the first time the American soldier took her into his arms right next to the potato bin, his wide shoulders shielding the frail glow of the ceiling bulb. That evening, and other evenings like it, the cement floor didn't feel cold at all through the blankets on which they lay.

At first she believed he'd take her with him after the war to his faraway country where the sky was always blue, where coconuts and oranges grew on trees, where winter never came and the ocean was warm. And because the wife he'd left there was a shadowy figure in Klara's mind, she assumed that, for him too, she had ceased to be real. Certainly he'd been apart from her for too long. Certainly it was Klara's touch, now, that mattered.

He didn't promise to take her with him, though she waited for him to say so, and when she stopped believing he ever would, she found comfort in the hope that the American occupation would last. He'd stay in Burgdorf, find work here or in Düsseldorf. Already his German had improved and she'd help him learn, practice with him.

The day she told him she was pregnant, he held her so tightly in his arms that she couldn't see the expression on his face, and then he kissed her, kissed her entire body, even the indentations her garters had left on her thighs. She wanted to see his face, but all she saw was herself through his eyes—a stretch of thigh, an instep, a breast, an arched neck, a moist strand of brown hair . . . and when his unit transferred him the next day—to Bochum, one of the American soldiers told her, while another said he was almost sure it was Duisburg—she was left with those fragments of herself to gather around a center that held the child growing within her.

She braced herself against her mother's silence and the disapproving stares of the townspeople. It was up to her to weave the story she would tell her son as soon as he started asking questions about his father.

But first there was the pain, the pain of being without her lover that took hold of her so fiercely she had trouble breathing, a pain that started deep inside her gut and spread into her limbs, her groin, a pain that racked her and tore her from deceptive moments of rest. It hurt so much she didn't know how to stop it. And out of the pain grew the fear that it would always be like this. Nothing helped. Not the crying. Not the praying. Not the confessing of her sins. The one person who could have stopped the pain was out of her reach.

When, finally, she became angry enough to crumple the one photo she had of him and throw it out, she retrieved it less than an hour later and ironed its back to take out the creases; but they stayed, a fine web across his face as though he had suddenly and irrevocably aged. All at once she had a vision of him as an old man, still tall but slightly stooped, and of herself, older too, one hand linked through his arm. She touched her unlined skin, ran her fingertips along the smooth planes of her cheeks, and cried out with the loss of all those years she would not spend with him.

She hid the photo in a red leather box under her few pieces of costume jewelry. After her son was born, she kept searching his features for a resemblance to the American, but only saw herself: the brown eyes and hair; the small, eager face; the flat, well-shaped ears. To protect the child from her shame, she insisted on being called Frau Brocker instead of Fräulein, the title reserved for unmarried women. And the townspeople complied; they even began to think of her as Frau Brocker, but they wouldn't forget that her child had come from sin.

Though the pain faded until it eventually ceased to be, the shame settled somewhere low in her belly, a familiar presence that claimed any food she ate before it could nourish her. Standing alone in the dim cellar after the potato man had left, she felt it stronger than she had in years. She looked at the wooden bin, at the cloud of fine dust that still floated above its open top, and she knew she was done with waiting, waiting for things that never happened.

She squatted in front of the bin. With both hands she shoved up the trap door, letting the old potatoes tumble out among dry specks that rose and swirled around the light bulb like fireflies, and as the potatoes rolled into dark corners, she caught the first new ones in her hands. They were firm, smooth.

"What are you doing?" Her son stood in the open cellar door. His brown hair hung over his eyebrows. His eyes were so serious. Too serious.

"Here!" She tossed one of the potatoes at him. "Catch!"

His hand snatched it from the air. "What—"

She laughed. "For dinner."

He seemed startled.

"Here—another one."

As Rolf caught the second one too, his lips moved into a

slow smile. He kicked aside an old potato that had rolled up against his feet.

"I'll boil them," she said, "and you can run to the store and get a quarter pound of butter. No—half a pound. And parsley." Already she could taste the new potatoes the way she would prepare them, and as her arms gathered as many as she could hold against herself, she felt the old hunger shrink into a small circle of desire.

✐ Props for Faith

W hen our housekeeper told me she didn't think the midwife was Renate's real mother, I wondered if my best friend's parents were gypsies, those dark-haired women and men who, every July, set up the carnival on the Burgdorf fairgrounds and, with brown, ring-covered hands, took the groschen I'd saved for rides on the ferris wheel and pink clouds of cotton candy. *Gypsies.* That would explain Renate's dark, frizzy hair, her quick, black eyes. But gypsies moved rapidly, while my friend walked with a limp, her feet in patent-leather shoes, her fragile ankles hidden under white knee socks that never stayed up.

Besides—gypsies were known to steal babies.

Not give them away.

After swearing me to secrecy, Frau Brocker told me, "I figure her real parents were too poor to keep her. Too many other children already." She'd just come back from her weekly visit to the beauty parlor and she smelled of hair spray. "Instead of paying the midwife, they must have given her the baby."

The midwife was a blond, heavy widow whose husband had been killed during the war on the Russian front. She'd delivered me and most of the kids I knew. Her name was Hilde Eberhardt, and she lived with her older son, Adi, and Renate in a white stucco house two blocks from school. No one had seen her pregnant with Renate, not even Trudi Montag. Twelve years before the midwife had left town one Thursday, and the following day she had returned with a dark-haired infant girl, claiming it was hers. By then her son had lived half of his five years without a father.

Renate didn't come to our school until the end of second grade, and we became best friends right away. Nearly two years earlier, she'd been taken to the Theresienheim with pneumonia. On the day she was to be released, she fell when she climbed out of bed, caved in on herself like a puppet whose strings had been cut. The nuns suspected polio and rushed her to St. Lukas hospital in Düsseldorf where the doctors confirmed the diagnosis and kept her for over a year, probing her legs with needles. Though she was eventually cured, her left leg was shorter than the other. Thinner. Both legs were pale with large pores.

Whenever Renate took me to her house, the midwife examined the soles of our shoes and followed us around with a mop, catching any speck of dust that dropped from our skirts and settled on her glossy parquet floor. Yet, when I got ready to leave, she'd say, "Come back, Hanna. Any time."

Their yard, too, was orderly: a lush lawn without dandelions; window boxes with forget-me-nots and geraniums; a trimmed hedge of purple lilacs. The one imperfection was a pear tree that produced abundant blossoms but only yielded hard little pears with brown spots.

With his blond hair and blue eyes, Renate's brother, Adi, didn't look anything like Renate. His full name was Adolf, but no one called him that. Quite a few boys in the grades above us were called Adolf—a name that had been popular for babies born in the early war years—but we had no Adolfs in our class or in the younger grades. The name

Adolf Hitler was never mentioned in our history classes. Our teachers dealt in detail with the old Greeks and Romans; we'd slowly wind our way up to Attila the Hun, to Henry the Eighth who had six wives, to Kaiser Wilhelm, to the First World War; from there we'd slide right back to the old Greeks and Romans.

In gym class Renate was always the last in line—awkward, hesitant, everything about her slow except for those dark eyes that seemed to move right through me. But I hardly thought about the polio or her leg until Sybille Immers, the butcher's daughter, called Renate a gimp one day as we left school. I leapt at Sybille, who was taller and heavier than I, kicking her shins; she raked her fingernails across my face and tore at my hair. When Frau Buttgereit, our music teacher, pulled us apart, her green hat with the pheasant feather fell into a puddle.

I still can't understand what I did less than a week later when Renate didn't want to come out and play.

"Why not?" I shouted, standing outside her bedroom window.

She leaned on the windowsill with both hands, "Because," she shouted back.

"Because why?"

"Because Sybille is coming over."

The scratches on my face still itched, and there she was, looking for a new best friend. Something hot and sad and mean rose inside me and, before I could stop myself, I yelled, "Even the gypsies didn't want to keep a gimp like you!"

Her arms tight against her body, Renate stood motionless. Her face turned red, then ashen.

I stared at her, horrified by what I had said. My throat ached, and when I tried to talk, I couldn't bring out one word.

"Hanna!" the side door slammed and the midwife ran toward me, her eyes filled with tears. "Don't you ever come back here," she shouted and raised one hand. "You hear me, Hanna?"

"But I didn't mean it," I cried out as I ran from her.

"I didn't mean it," I told Renate in school the next day, but she said she wasn't allowed to play with me anymore and walked away.

Her limp seemed worse than ever before, and I felt as if I had caused it. If only I could take back the words. During recess, she stood alone in the school yard, eating an apple. My hands in the pockets of my pleated skirt, I leaned against the fence close by, feeling hollow despite the cheese sandwich I'd just eaten. If only she'd call me something real bad, something worse than gimp. Even if she said that my parents had found me at the dump, or that my mother should have thrown me away as a baby because I was too ugly to keep—I pushed my fists deeper into my pockets, jammed back my elbows into the diamond-shaped holes in the fence.

After school I waited for her outside the building. "Do you want to buy some licorice?"

She shook her head.

"I still have my allowance."

"I'm not hungry."

"We could ride bikes."

"I have to go home." She crossed the street.

I followed her on the opposite sidewalk. Mist hung low above the streets and garden walls, yet left the trees and houses untouched. Frau Weskopp passed us on her bicycle, her black coat flapping around her. I could tell she was on her way to the cemetery because a watering can dangled from her handlebar. When Renate reached her front door, she turned around as if she wanted to make sure I was close by before she slipped inside.

I left my books at our house and walked toward the river. The streets were damp; it had rained nearly every day that April. When I got close to the Tegerns' house, the architect's seven German shepherds threw themselves against the chain-link fence, barking. The skin above their gums were drawn back, and their teeth glistened. Though Renate and I always ran past the fence, I made myself stop on the sidewalk, close enough to smell the wet fur and see the strings of saliva on the dog's tongues. I snarled back at them. The hair on their backs rose as they scrambled across each other, trying to climb up the fence, barking and howling at me.

"Cowards," I hissed, wishing Renate could see me. I raised my hands, curled my fingers into claws. "Cowards."

A curtain shifted in the window above the solarium and Frau Tegern knocked against the glass, motioning me away as if afraid for me or, perhaps, herself. I gave the dogs one final ferocious growl and turned my back to them.

Along the river the mist was thicker, and the water looked brown-green, darker than the meadow where a herd of sheep grazed. I heard the tearing of grass blades as their teeth closed around them. The shapes of poplars and willows were blurred. Above the water line the rocks were gray and damp, the upper ones splotched with a white crust.

Frau Brocker used to bring Rolf and me to the river when we were small. While she smoked one of her Gauloises, Rolf and I searched for scraps of paper and dry leaves, packing them into the crevices between the stones before setting a match to them.

I sat on a boulder and dug my sneakers into the heaps of pebbles around me. Maybe if I gave Renate a present . . . I could let her have my radio. Or any of the dolls in my

room. I didn't play with them anyhow. But neither did
Renate. I picked up a pebble, tried to flit it across the
waves; it sank without rising once. Perhaps we could
switch bicycles. She liked mine better than hers. It had
even been touched by holy water at the pastor's last blessing of the vehicles and didn't have any rust on it.

If I were Renate, the thing I'd want most in the world—
it was so simple—her leg, of course, her left leg, to have it
grow and fill out like the other one. I thought of my Oma's
healer—not even a saint—who'd touched her leg and dissolved a blood clot in the artery below her knee. Oma had
told me it was as much her belief in the healing as the
healing itself that had saved her leg from having to be amputated. Miracles happened that way. Even without saints.
As long as you believed in them. I bent to search for a flat,
round pebble and found a white one with amber veins.
After spitting on it for luck, I skipped it across the water.
It sprang up in wide arcs four, five . . . a total of eight
times.

That evening I looked around our cellar for an empty
bottle. Our housekeeper stored things there which she said
she might use some day: cardboard boxes with old magazines and brochures, empty bottles and jars, a four-liter pot
with a hole in the bottom, a stained lampshade, even the
tin tub I'd been bathed in until I was two. Most of the
bottles were too large, but finally I found an empty vinegar
bottle behind the washing machine.

I soaked off the label, rinsed the inside, and hid it in my
room until Wednesday morning when St. Martin's Church
was empty because mass was held at the chapel. The bottle
in my knapsack, I sneaked into the side door of the church
early before school. In the morning light the blond wood
of the pews gleamed as if someone had rubbed it with oil.
The stale scent of incense made it hard to breathe. Though

I knew Herr Pastor Beier was at the chapel two kilometers away, I kept glancing toward the purple curtains of the confessional.

Marble steps with a red runner led to the altar, which was built of solid black marble. Centered between two silver bowls with tulips stood five candles thicker than Renate's legs. From *The Last Supper* mural above the altar, the dark eyes of Jesus and the apostles traced my movements. I'd heard enough stories about church robbers to know the wrath of God could strike at any moment and leave me dead on the floor. As I walked toward the back of the church to the basin of holy water, the white veins in the marble floor reached for my feet like the nets of a fisherman.

Quickly I submerged my vinegar bottle in the cold water. Silver bubbles rose to the surface as the bottle filled —much too slowly. On the wide balcony above me, I felt the silent weight of the organ pipes.

"You want to come to my house?" I whispered to Renate as I followed her out of school that afternoon.

She shook her head and kept walking, tilting to the left with each step, her white knee socks bunched around her ankles.

"It's about a surprise."

She glanced at me sideways. "What is it?"

"I can't tell." My knapsack over one arm, I continued walking next to her. "I have to show it to you."

"Why?"

"Because. It's a secret."

"What if I don't want it?"

"You will. I swear."

She stopped. "Is it a harmonica?"

"Better."

"Better than a kitten?"

"Much better."

"Better than—"

"The best thing that could happen to you," I promised.

She still had some doubt in her eyes as we took the steps down to our cellar. I thought of the nights my mother and grandmother had hidden there with neighbors while the wail of sirens pierced the dark. The war had ended a year before Renate and I were born. Several kids in our school had lost their fathers at the Russian front. Adults never mentioned the war unless we asked about it, and then they fled into vague sentences about a dark period for Germany. "Nobody wants to relive those years," they'd say gravely. My mother was the only one who answered some of our questions and told us about the terror of air raids, the hunger and cold everyone had suffered.

"Sit over there." I pointed to the crates next to the apple shelves. Every fall my father and I filled those crates with apples we'd picked at an orchard in Krefeld. Afterward we'd wrap the apples in newspaper and lay them on the shelves. It was my job to rotate them every two weeks, sorting out the rotten ones, so the others would last through the winter.

Renate sat on the crate closest to the door. The wall at the far end of the cellar was still black, right up to the two high windows that were blind with layers of coal dust and cobwebs. Until the oil furnace had been installed two years before, I used to help my father stack coal briquets to within a hand's width of the window.

I picked up the other crate and moved it in front of Renate. "You have to take off your left shoe and sock."

"Why?" She straightened her shoulders.

"Because. It's part of it. You'll see." I took the bottle from my knapsack.

Renate pulled her bare foot from the cement floor. "It's cold."

I sat down on the crate across from her. "Let me have

your leg." When she hesitated, I whispered, "I've figured out a way to make it all right—your leg, I mean—heal it."

She swallowed hard. "How?"

"It'll be like your other leg."

She drew her lower lip between her teeth, but then she raised her left leg and, carefully, laid her bare foot on my knees. It was a pale foot, a thin foot with toenails longer than mine, a foot that felt warm and sweaty as I put one hand around it to keep her from yanking it back.

With my teeth I uncorked the bottle. "All you need to do is close your eyes and believe it will work."

"What's in there?" Renate stared at me.

"Holy water." I poured some of it into my palm. It felt cold and smelled musty.

"Wait." She reached into her mouth with her right fore-finger and thumb and took out a pink wad of chewing gum. After sticking it on the side of her crate, she closed her eyes and raised her face as though about to receive communion.

I rubbed the holy water up and down Renate's calf, be-tween her toes, along the arch of her foot. Light filtered in uneven splotches from the dust-smeared light bulb above us. I've always had an enormous capacity to believe. Sto-ries, miracles, lies—with the right details, I can be con-vinced of the authenticity of nearly anything, even *Hasenbrot*, rabbit bread, which my father brought me many evenings when he returned from working on people's teeth. Handing me half a sandwich wrapped in oil-stained brown paper, he'd tell me that on his way home he'd seen a *Hase*, a rabbit, by the side of the road, carrying this package— he'd motion to the sandwich—between its front paws. He leapt from his car to catch it, but the *Hase* ran off with the bundle; my father followed it across the brook and chased it along Schreberstrasse until the *Hase* finally dropped the package next to the brook and disappeared. The bundle was about to slide into the water when my father saw it.

Every time my father chased the *Hase* through a different

area, and every time there was that one breath-catching
moment when the bundle was almost lost all over again
because a car nearly ran over it or a dog tried to tear it from
his hands. I'd unfold the brown paper with something bor-
dering on reverence. Though the bread was always a bit
stale, the meat limp, and the cheese soggy, I've never tasted
anything as delicious as my father's *Hasenbrot*.

And it was with that kind of faith that I dribbled holy
water over Renate's foot and leg. I kneaded it into the cres-
cent-shaped callus at her heel, into the bony disk of her
knee. Her teeth had released her lower lip, and she
breathed evenly.

Already I felt a difference in her leg: the skin seemed
warmer and didn't look as pale anymore. With each day
her leg would stretch itself, grow fuller, stronger. It would
be able to keep up with the other leg when she pedaled her
bike. She'd play hopscotch. Tag.

"You can look now."

Renate blinked, staring at me, then at her leg.

"See?" I bent over her leg, my heart fast.

Cautiously she probed her ankle with her fingertips, then
her calf. "I think so."

"It's already begun to change."

"Are you sure?"

"Absolutely."

"Should we do it again tomorrow? To make double
sure?"

"No," I said, instinctively knowing the difference between a miracle and a treatment. "All you need to do is
believe it worked."

She raised her leg from my knees. "It feels different."

"See?"

"What do we do with the rest of the holy water?"

I hadn't even thought of that. The bottle was still half
full. It didn't feel right to pour it out or leave it here in the
basement.

"We could drink it," Renate suggested.

I felt as if the eyes of the apostles were watching me as I raised the bottle to my lips, swallowed, and gave it to Renate who drank and handed it back to me. It tasted the way damp stones smell and within an hour I had stomach cramps, punishment, no doubt, for stealing holy water, a sin I didn't dare confess.

Over the next weeks I watched for signs of change in Renate's left leg. I pictured the pores closing, the skin losing its chalky color, the calf filling out.

"Does it feel different?" I'd ask her, and she'd nod and say, "I think so."

The end of April we took our bicycles to the annual blessing of vehicles on the Burgdorf fairgrounds where Herr Pastor Beier sprinkled holy water on cars, trucks, tractors, motor scooters, and bikes to keep them in good condition and out of accidents. Renate still couldn't keep up with me as we rode back to her house. By then the midwife had accepted my apology and welcomed me back into her house, all the time cleaning up behind us.

In July Renate and I picked purple clover blossoms on the fairgrounds and watched the gypsies set up their tents and booths. I found myself staring at their faces, afraid to discover resemblances between Renate and them, relieved when I didn't. We rode the merry-go-round, ate white sausages with mustard, threw Ping-Pong balls through wooden loops. The biggest tent had been set up for the circus, and Renate's mother took Adi and us to the Saturday performance. We applauded when five fat clowns tumbled out of a tiny car, when the animal tamer stuck his head inside the lion's mouth, and when the elephants circled the arena, their trunks holding the tails of the elephants ahead of them.

During intermission Adi bought us candied apples, and

when we returned to our seats, the lights dimmed. It turned dark inside the tent, and the voices faded into whispers, then silence. High above us a slow shimmer began to spread. It came from a woman with black hair who stood on the tightrope in a short golden dress. I felt Renate's hand on my arm; her fingers were dry, warm. The woman's arms and legs shimmered as she set one foot in front of the other and crossed the wide gap.

If there were nets that day in the circus, Renate and I didn't see them. We believed the woman was safe. It had to do with faith. We had proven that to ourselves that afternoon in the cellar when the holy water had worked after all, not healing Renate's leg but the rift between us. Some acts of faith, I believe, have the power to grant us something infinitely wiser than what we imagine. We all have our props for faith, and the shakier the faith, the more props we need. But sometimes the faith is strong enough so that an old vinegar bottle with holy water and a crate next to the apple shelves will do.

✐ My Father's Reckless Act

"**D**on't tell your parents you heard this from me," Trudi Montag whispered, "but your father was engaged when he met your mother."

We stood on the fairgrounds with our bicycles, surrounded by hundreds of people who were waiting for Herr Pastor Beier's blessing of the vehicles. Since Renate was sick in bed with the measles, I'd pushed my bike next to Trudi Montag, who liked to arrive early to get a space in front where some of the sacred sprinkles would land on the child's bicycle she used. She'd bought it before I was born with some of the money her Aunt Helene used to smuggle to her from America during the war, hidden inside spools of thread. She'd remove the round label at one end, roll up the money, and push it into the hollow core of the spool before gluing the label back on.

"The woman's name was Brigitte Raudschuss. She was a teacher. The daughter of Wilhelm Raudschuss, that rich lawyer in Oberkassel?" It came out like a question.

I shook my head, too stunned to answer.

"She was getting along in years . . . around your father's

age when he proposed. And he wasn't so young either. He must have been—mid-thirties, at least?"

"He was thirty-six when he married my mother."

"Who was nineteen, I know, nearly half his age." Trudi Montag smiled. "Anyhow, your father's wedding with Brigitte Raudschuss was set two months away when your mother came to his office to have a filling replaced. . . ."

That part of the story I knew from my father. Although he'd never mentioned Brigitte Raudschuss to me, he'd told me about that afternoon when he'd fallen in love with my mother. She'd come in late for her appointment because she'd been painting the Sternburg. Carrying her easel and paints, she arrived at his office when he was about to lock up. Though he'd taken care of her teeth before, he'd never really looked at her, at least not the way he looked at her that hot, late day in June when her blond hair was tangled and her skin flushed from running. Strands of damp hair clung to her forehead and neck. She was a student at the Art Academy in Düsseldorf.

He let himself be convinced to keep his office open for her although his assistant had already left for the day. "But only if you let me have a look at your painting," he told her.

"I had to finish it before the light changed."

He held her picture of the Sternburg with both hands and, silently, gazed at the layers of light that illuminated the draw bridge, the moat where bright red leaves floated like rose petals, the baroque tower that grew into the cloudless sky.

". . . and within five weeks they were married," Trudi Montag said, "an earlier wedding date than the one he'd set with Brigitte Raudschuss. Brigitte's father, the lawyer, even came to Burgdorf one morning."

"What happened?"

"His car was parked outside your father's office for an hour and twenty minutes. But whatever he said didn't make any difference because your father married your mother the next week."

Herr Pastor Beier walked across the fairgrounds, followed by two altar boys. One of them swung the thurible back and forth on its silver chain to let the incense rise into the moist air; the other carried the boat for the incense and the silver bucket with holy water. I'd heard of car engines that had lost their coughs after the blessing, of tractors that had been rusty until they'd been touched with holy water, of bicycle tires that had leaked air until Herr Pastor had blessed them.

"Have you seen her since then . . . Brigitte Raudschuss?" I asked Trudi Montag.

She shrugged. "A few times. Never got married though I hear there was one fellow who proposed. Worked for her father. As far as I know she still teaches in Oberkassel."

Almost everyone I knew had come to the fairgrounds for the annual blessing: Frau Weiler and Frau Wilhelmini had full shopping nets hanging from the handlebars of their bicycles; the Hansen bakery truck stood between the town's fire engine and the delivery truck from Becker's grocery store; Albert Zimmermann, the painter, leaned against his motorcycle, which gleamed as if he had polished it for hours; Frau Behrmeier, who used to be my second-grade teacher, sat in her car with Frau Buttgereit, our music teacher, who wore one of her awful hats—the purple one with the two peacock feathers; Karin Baum was there with a new white bicycle—probably from her grandfather's store.

My parents had bought my bicycle in Düsseldorf. They wouldn't speak to Karin's grandfather who owned the only bicycle shop in Burgdorf. Sometimes I missed being friends with Karin. Until we were both seven, we used to play together every day, but because of her grandfather, I

was no longer allowed to go to her apartment. His shop
was downstairs in the house where Karin lived, and it was
a filthy place—that's what my mother had said.

Karin's long brown braid swung across her shoulder as
she turned in my direction, perhaps aware that I was
watching her, and I waved to her. She raised her hand and
looked away.

"Falling in love with your mother," Trudi Montag said,
"was the one reckless act your father committed in his life,
and he has lived since then as if to make up for it."

I worked the tip of my right shoe into the dry ground,
loosening a small rock. The sky was leaden except for shifting streaks of pearl where the clouds thinned out and let
the sun through. By July this whole field would be covered
with clover, buttercups, and dandelions. Gypsies would
appear with their tents and cotton candy, their fat lady and
fortune-teller. Renate and I would ride the merry-go-round
and ferris wheel, win fuzzy animals at the shooting booth,
and dare each other to keep our eyes open inside the
haunted house.

"I can see why he fell in love with her," Trudi Montag
said. "Even if she is a little . . . wild, your mother is beautiful. And tall," she added with a sigh that made me won-
der how often she'd wished her body would stretch itself
and grow. "But I still haven't figured out why she married
him. She could have had any man."

Perhaps my mother liked the way my father's gray eyes
rested on her face as if he were trying to memorize it;
perhaps she liked how his full beard curled back from the
tender outline of his lips; or perhaps she sensed that he'd
always understand her need to paint.

"Any man she wanted." Trudi Montag nodded.

Sometimes my father seemed baffled by my mother,
worried about the risks she would take, while she became
impatient with him. Yet, whenever he visited her studio,

they stood close together as they looked at her newest painting, and when I went with them for walks in the Grafenberg Forest, they held hands.

"But she picked my father," I said to Trudi Montag.

Herr Pastor Beier made his way along our row. In his left hand he held a silver handle with a ball at one end. While his right hand drew the sign of the cross, he dipped the handle into the bucket and swished it through the air, sprinkling us and our bicycles with holy water that escaped from the ball's tiny holes.

My mother didn't believe in the blessings. She had stopped going to church when my brother, Joachim, had died. My father was the one who went to mass with me every Sunday and who used to read me the Joseph story from the Bible until I'd learned to read on my own. Sitting on his knees, I had listened to him read my favorite story about Joseph who saw meaning in dreams, whose brothers sold him to the Egyptians and didn't see him again until he'd interpreted the Pharoah's dreams and saved Egypt from famine.

Moments after the drops of holy water touched us, they merged with splatters of rain that plastered Trudi Montag's white curls to her forehead and soaked my skirt and blouse. Herr Pastor Beier walked faster, blessing three or four ve-hicles at a time. Water ran from his round face like tears and splotched the purple chasuble that stuck out in front of his belly. He liked food more than anyone I knew. One Easter he'd devoured Rolf's chocolate bunny and most of his colored eggs. His eyes had glazed over with satisfaction, reminding me of infants who forget everything around them when they're fed.

Trudi Montag and I rode our bikes to her pay-library where Anton Immers, the butcher's father, stood outside the locked door with an umbrella, waiting to check out a new nurse-and-doctor novel. An old man with distrustful eyes, he finished at least two books a week; yet, when he returned them, he always complained that they hadn't been as interesting as the ones he had read before.

"Didn't see you at the blessing," Trudi Montag said.

He grumbled something to himself and shuffled toward the bookshelves. While he read jacket flaps, I went into the bathroom, dried my hair, and wrung out my plaid skirt above the tub. On the inside of the door hung a long mirror. I wondered how Trudi Montag felt when she climbed out of the tub and saw the reflection of her stunted body. Did she ever get used to it? Or did she need to turn her back toward her image as she dried herself?

That evening, when my mother tucked me in, she wore her watered-silk gown and had braided her hair into a soft double coil at the nape of her neck. She and my father were on their way to see *Aida* at the Düsseldorf *Opernhaus* where they had a subscription. Each time he bought her a box of sugar-coated almonds in the lobby of the *Opernhaus*. They were pink and glossy, and she saved most of them for me. I always made them last as long as possible, letting them dissolve in my mouth, anticipating the moment when the pink taste would give way to the essence of the almond hidden deep within the sweet shell.

My mother sat down on the edge of the bed. She smelled of perfume and cigarette smoke.

I ran one finger across the crisp silk of her skirt. "Why did you marry Dad?"

"Now where did that come from?"

I shrugged.

"I know why he married me." She gave me a mischievous smile. "So he could have my painting of the Sternburg. First he asked if it was for sale, and when I said no, he figured he'd better marry me."

"That day . . . did he drill your tooth?"

She nodded.

"Did it hurt?"

"He was careful."

I felt cheated. My father had always sent me to another dentist. "I don't want to be the one to hurt you," he'd tell me. Still, I felt enraged whenever I flinched under the drill of Dr. Beck, convinced my father would be gentler. I felt excluded when Karin Baum and Renate went to him, even Frau Talmeister, who lived across the street and was one of my father's worst patients. "She starts shaking before I turn on the drill," he said. Yet even she would answer, "Not much," when I asked her if my father ever hurt her.

"But that was the last time he worked on my teeth," my mother told me. She too had to go to Dr. Beck with his wide chin and those black hairs inside his nostrils.

I wished I could ask her about Brigitte Raudschuss—if she'd ever met her, if she was tall like my mother, if she liked peach pie.

"Remember, lights out at nine." As she bent to kiss me, the silk of her gown swished against my arm. "I'll see you in the morning."

"And you'll bring me almonds?"

"Don't I always?" she asked, and I knew that, when I woke up, I'd find a glossy box with almonds on my night table, certain proof that my parents had slipped into my room while I was asleep.

After my parents left, I retrieved the current romance novel Frau Brocker had hidden under the cover of the ironing board. The folded tissue, which she kept as a bookmark, was only between the pages 73 and 74. I was already on page 145. But I couldn't concentrate on the story of the heiress who was betrayed by her aunt and rescued by a baron. I kept wondering what I would be like if my father had married Brigitte Raudschuss and if she were my mother. A teacher, Trudi Montag had said. *She's in school while I'm in a classroom down the hall. In the afternoons we do things together. She likes books, sledding on the dike in the winter, hot chocolate, walks along the river. . . .*

But if my father had married Brigitte Raudschuss, I would have never been born or—at least—I would have been someone entirely different. I tried to imagine him with her, a quiet woman closer to him in age, and all at once I felt strange as though I'd done something to hurt my mother.

"Falling in love with your mother was the one reckless act your father committed in his life. . . ."

I'd never thought of my father as reckless, though it was a word he used when he cautioned my mother against driving so fast or swimming nude in the ocean. Every summer, when we rented a cottage on the island Wangerooge in the North Sea, my father refused to let me swim out with my mother.

"It's too deep, Hanna," he told me while my mother turned her back to the beach and the crowds that kept near the sandy crescents. Alone out there in the deep, she took off her bathing suit and swam, holding the straps in the crook of one elbow.

"You might lose it," my father warned her, but she told him she liked the feel of the waves against her bare skin.

One day my father was proven right: the sea tore my mother's red swimsuit from her arm, and though she tried to dive for it, she couldn't find it in the green-clear water that stung her eyes. She stayed out there, swimming farther away whenever others came near her. She kept waving to me and my father, and we waved back.

"I bet she finally did it—lost her swimsuit," my father said. Grabbing his beach towel, he held it up.

Way out there, my mother nodded, motioning him toward her.

My father shook his head, but then he laughed. His

towel in one hand, he ran into the North Sea, and when I followed him, he called out to me, "Stay right there, Hanna. Only up to your knees."

Waves slapped against my thighs as I watched him swim toward my mother. I stood on my toes, trying to see their heads when he reached her, but they disappeared between the waves and then bobbed up together on white crests. I walked to where the water covered my waist. For a long time my parents stayed out there, and sometimes their heads were so close they looked like one shape. When they walked out of the water, the towel which my mother clasped around her was so heavy with sea water that she had to hold it up with both hands. Her hair covered her shoulders as if molded from one sheet of brass.

"Next time all you get is a washcloth." My father smiled at her.

She touched one finger to his lips. Drops of salt water glistened in his reddish beard, filling it with specks of light.

The clock on my bookshelf showed a quarter to ten. My parents wouldn't be home for at least another hour. I tried to read another page of the romance novel though my eyelids felt heavy. The light from the lamp on my bedside table painted a yellow circle on the ceiling. It was quiet in our apartment, a silence that had a texture of its own, a different texture than when my parents were asleep and their breaths—even though I couldn't hear them—took the starch out of the cloth of silence and made it smooth like a familiar blanket.

But when I was alone, the cloth of silence was always new, and it could be exciting, boring—even eerie. Most of the time I enjoyed it. I could stay up longer than I was allowed to; I could read Frau Brocker's trashy novels; I could sit on my windowsill and write lists of suspicious persons. When my parents were home, the light in my

room had to be out by nine, but I often read afterwards
with a flashlight under my blanket. A few times my father
had caught me, but the punishment—early bedtime the
next evening—was well worth all the nights I wasn't
caught.

I hid the book under my pillow, switched off the light,
and pulled my blanket higher. As I shut my eyes, I wondered what Brigitte Raudschuss would have done had she
lost her bathing suit. But she probably wouldn't have taken
it off. She'd swim next to the shore. She'd listen to my
father's warning. She'd be cautious enough not to need any
warnings.

Reckless—I rather liked that about my father, and from
that night on, I found myself thinking of him in a different
way. As I imagined him in other reckless acts, I discovered
in him the touch of daring I'd only connected to my
mother. Marrying a woman who was reckless must have
been the ultimate reckless act, requiring a lifetime of bal-
ancing to keep both of them safe.

The Order of Punishment

Our tenant, Matthias Berger, who rented the third-floor apartment next to my mother's studio, was given to sudden violent headaches that made his hands rise to his temples and his fingers press against the fair skin as if he were trying to squeeze out the pain and connect his palms in a prayer of absolution. I'd see the headache behind his eyes, a dark shape that sucked the green from his eyes.

I met Matthias the day he moved into our house; his piano got stuck where our staircase bent between the second and third floors, and the movers threatened to leave it there after struggling with it for half an hour. On the landing above the piano stood Matthias, a blond man with solid shoulders, tugging at one of the piano legs as if he believed it would make a difference. And it did—the bulky instrument moved slowly, leaving deep scars in the plaster wall as the movers wedged their bodies against it and Matthias pulled. His glasses were plain, but even on the dim staircase his eyes were a splendid green with gold flecks.

The next afternoon I found him on the stairs with a knife, spreading white paste into the gashes his piano had torn into the wall. He looked at me with those splendid eyes and continued patching the holes. Except for the scraping of the knife against plaster, it was silent around us. Downstairs in our apartment, Frau Brocker was canning beans and their fart smell drifted past us. Once, a door opened on the second floor, then closed with a thud. I sat three steps above Matthias, watching his long hands, his face, and it was as if we were talking, finding out things about each other though neither of us said a word, and somehow I knew he was filled with a light he would only let very few people see.

When he closed the jar of paste, he smiled at me. "I'm Matthias," he said, and his voice was warm and low, just as I had imagined it.

"I'm Hanna."

"Hanna," he said as if trying out the name, matching it against me, as I sat on the stairs above him, at the same level with his gold-flecked eyes. "Do you like lemonade, Hanna?"

Matthias asked me to call him by his first name. He made lemonade for me that afternoon and opened a box of chocolate-covered hazelnuts.

"Don't you want any?" I asked after I'd finished about half of them and felt a sweet-queasy sensation that would turn into a stomachache if I didn't stop.

"I never eat them," he said.

He was an orderly in the Theresienheim, the hospital run by the sisters on Römerstrasse where, twelve years before, Sister Ingeborg had pronounced me dead. When I told Matthias, he said he knew Sister Ingeborg—she'd hired him to work in the old people's wing where, as the one male employee, it was his job to turn over those old people in their beds who were too heavy for the nuns.

In her pay-library Trudi Montag whispered to me that his other job was to bathe the old men. "To keep the nuns from going blind," she said and laughed. "I heard he was in a seminary in Kaiserslautern until two years ago." She handed me two romance novels that belonged on a shelf too high for her to reach. "To become a priest."

I reached up and jammed the books among equally colorful jackets. "Why did he leave?"

"Maybe he got kicked out."

"Or maybe he just didn't want to stay."

Yet, I still had to ask him. The only priest I knew was Herr Pastor Beier, who celebrated mass every Sunday and heard confessions on Saturday. The day of my first communion he had told me and the other children as we knelt there—the girls in white dresses, the boys in blue suits—that this was the happiest day of our lives. I'd clutched the lace handkerchief my mother had wrapped around the stem of my communion candle, waiting for that promised happiness to take hold of me, but all I'd felt was a curious sense of letdown.

"Did you want to become a priest?" I asked Matthias.

"Who told you this?" He sat at his piano, playing a rapid sequence of notes I had never heard.

"Trudi Montag. She heard it—"

"—from someone else who heard it from someone else. . . ." He smiled. His hands kept gliding across the ivory keys. Then he closed his eyes as if trying to remember or—perhaps—forget something. Softly, like someone who'd been in pain for a long time, he said, "It became apparent that I wasn't chosen."

Above his window hung a wooden crucifix. Nails were hammered through Jesus's palms. His right foot rested above the left so that one nail could connect both feet to the cross. Ribs showed above the carved lines of the cloth he wore tied around his waist. The wood on top of his outstretched arms and in the hollows between his ribs looked lighter where dust had dulled the dark sheen of the wood.

Though Matthias was in his late twenties, his rooms held the smell of old skin, as though he had carried it home from the Theresienheim in his hair and on the soles of his shoes. I'd recognize his steps on the hallway stairs and wait a few minutes before rushing upstairs to knock on his door.

He always seemed glad to see me. His apartment was half dark as if the sun hurt his eyes—so different from my mother's studio next door, one huge room flooded with light. Once she'd invited Matthias to see her work, and he'd stood for a long time in front of one of her pictures of the Rhein, gazing at the streaks of sun that broke the waves into layers brighter than the sky.

"I didn't know anyone else saw the river like this," he finally said.

That evening, when my mother tucked me in, I asked if she liked Matthias.

She nodded, but then she said something that puzzled me. "He has made some difficult choices."

Matthias's apartment had the same amount of space as my mother's studio, but it was divided into three cramped rooms. Most of his living room was taken up by his piano, which he played for me, his long fingers gliding through Mozart's piano concertos and Schumann's etudes. He collected books of photographs from countries all over the world. In his apartment I saw the fjords of Norway, the great wall of China, the beaches of Bermuda, and the glaciers of the Italian Alps. On his walls he had Japanese charcoal drawings of birds and flowers. He talked about wanting to take a train south through Austria and into Italy, about flying to Japan or Africa.

"I can't imagine staying in Burgdorf forever," he said and ran his hands across the globe he'd set on top of the piano. "With all there is to see . . ."

He often walked as though he were tired, his limbs moving as though it cost him enormous effort—except when his friend Herr Faber came over with a bottle of wine or a box of chocolate-covered hazelnuts. Then his motions became hurried and he'd usher me out the door, glancing at his friend as if worried he might resent my being there.

Herr Faber was a violinist with the Düsseldorf Symphony Orchestra. He didn't like kids. I didn't know what he liked, because he looked so glum with his dark eyebrows and mustache. I wondered why Matthias kept inviting him; he always seemed unhappy after Herr Faber left. Sometimes, he'd have a bruise on one cheek or his arm; once, his right eye was swollen shut.

"It's nothing," he'd whisper when I asked. "I was careless."

But I knew his injuries had something to do with his friend, though I couldn't imagine Matthias fighting. I thought about telling my father so that he could forbid Herr Faber to come into our house, but I didn't ask for his help because I was afraid he might not let me see Matthias anymore.

One Saturday afternoon in July, after Herr Faber and Matthias had sent me away, I climbed the stairs to the attic. Lying flat on the dusty floor, I pressed one ear against the boards. From the rooms below, the sound of men's voices floated up, but the words did not separate themselves enough to distinguish; they drifted through like one huge blanket that settled around me, weighing me down. Herr Faber's voice was louder.

"Why do you let him come back?" I'd asked Matthias once when his left eye was swollen shut.

He'd winced as if I were the one who'd hurt him. "He's my friend, Hanna." He'd lifted his fingers to his forehead, and I'd seen the headache taking shape behind his eyes, dark and sudden.

I wondered if my mother could hear them in her studio, but the stairwell divided the two apartments. I pictured Herr Faber leaving and getting run over by a streetcar like Monika Klein, who'd been killed two years before when she and I were in the fourth grade. The wheels of the streetcar would cut across Herr Faber's chest or maybe his throat. Either way—he'd stop breathing. For a while Matthias would be sad, but I'd visit him, bring him travel books from the church library, and make us lemonade.

I got up and brushed off my wrinkled skirt. Walking over to the front window, I unlatched it and pushed it open. Sunlight streamed in, magnifying the motes of dust that circled me like a second skin. A pigeon with a straw in its beak flew off and landed in the cherry tree in front of the Talmeisters' house across the street. As usual, Frau Talmeister leaned from her living-room window, supported by a wide pillow. Propped on the sill next to her lay her eight-month-old son, Helmut. She fed him with a spoon, barely looking at him as if afraid she might miss something going on in the street. Our housekeeper had told me the only thing that kept Frau Talmeister from nursing the baby in the window was her fear of being arrested for indecent exposure.

For a moment there, something odd happened to me: from where I stood in the attic, I saw the side part in Frau Talmeister's curled hair, the white material of her blouse stretching across her shoulders; I also felt the metal spoon in her hand as she fed her son, felt his mouth opening and the skin on his throat shifting, tasted the bland oatmeal as he swallowed.

From St. Martin's Church came the swelling sound of the bells. Five o'clock. I stretched out my right arm and touched the level section of roof outside the window. The tiles felt warm against my palms. I thought of my great-uncle Alexander who had leapt from this window before I was born. A few months before I'd had a dream of him flying, arms stretched out, never touching the ground. When I told Matthias about it, he listened carefully.

"He may have been happy those few moments," he said

and smiled at me until I felt I would drown in his gold-flecked eyes, eyes more alive than the rest of him.

"Do you think he believed he was flying?" I asked.

"Maybe," he said. "Maybe that's what he needed to believe."

At the time I only nodded; now I wished I could ask Matthias what he'd meant by that, but he was with Herr Faber and wouldn't let me in if I knocked on his door. I had tried that once, and when he'd finally answered, he'd worn his sweater inside-out. He'd blinked at me. "You have to go home, Hanna."

I closed the attic window tight and went back to listen through the floorboards, but the voices from below had stopped. Sitting on the wooden trunk that was filled with my great-uncle's brittle silk ties and stiff woolens, I wished I were at the river with my mother. We'd skip flat pebbles across the surface, count the times they touched the water and raised themselves in perfect arcs. She often got eight, even twelve skips, before the pebbles sank. One of my pebbles had made it eleven times, the most ever for me.

In the corner stood the wicker baby carriage my mother had used to take me for walks. It was in some of my baby photos, white and new, but now the wicker was yellow and its crevices were embedded with old dirt like a farmer's fingernails. The spokes of the wheels had rusted, and when I pushed the carriage back and forth, it squeaked.

A young couple, the Wienens, used to live in the apartment below until they had a baby and needed a larger place. Matthias had heard about it from Frau Wienen's father who lived in the Theresienheim, and he'd come to our house to ask if he could rent the apartment. Until then he'd shared a small walk-up on Lindenstrasse with another man. My mother, who had inherited the building from her uncle Alexander, didn't have to advertise vacancies. Apartments were so scarce that she'd receive dozens of inquiries if someone was planning to move out, and if someone died people would phone about the apartment before the funeral had even taken place.

Through Matthias's eyes, I'd begun to see our house and the backyard in a different way, had come to see its limitations. Built flush to the sidewalk, the building, which my great-uncle had built in the shape of an L, blocked the sunlight from the backyard. When I was little, I had played there with Manfred Weiler, who lived in the other arm of the L. We'd ridden our tricycles on the hard-packed dirt, bumping into the fence to see how far the chain links would bounce us back. Surrounded by too many windows, we had no privacy, just as, according to Matthias, there couldn't be any privacy when you shared a connecting wall between buildings. It didn't matter how thick they were; it didn't matter that they were built of cinder blocks and bricks and mortar—to him they were no more than a sham.

"What a difference it would make," he told me once, "to live in a house that stands by itself, to know that on the other side of my bedroom wall are trees and grass."

From below came the sound of a door closing. My fingers tightened on the handlebar of the baby carriage. Maybe Herr Faber had heard the squeaking wheels. Maybe he was coming up here to yell at me or worse. But the steps on the stairs moved away from me, growing fainter until I only heard the pulse of my blood inside my ears. I pictured Herr Faber's hand brushing against the wall where Matthias had filled the scars his piano had left, scars you couldn't see if you didn't know where they were, but if your fingers happened to move across them, they felt smoother than the texture of the wall.

I wanted to run down to Matthias's apartment, talk with him, but I couldn't bring myself to look at him, afraid he would carry new bruises. Instead I stood outside my mother's studio, wondering if I should interrupt her. Finally I knocked and she opened the door for me, one of my father's old shirts over her dress.

"Hanna," she said but looked at me as if trying to remember who I was. She got like that when she painted, forgetting everyone and everything around her except the work and the movement of colors from her heart to the canvas.

"Can I watch?"

"Of course." She smiled and turned her back to me.

I closed the door and followed her to the window. On her easel stood a new picture of the Sternburg, the old castle she'd painted many times. For the baroque tower she'd chosen a deep blue. With her brush she set silver clouds of mosquitoes on the canvas. They floated above the moat where leaves drifted, weightless shapes in bright colors. I wished she would lay her brush aside, sit down with me.

"It's beautiful . . . the painting," I whispered, touching my mother's sleeve, but she didn't see me.

I don't know why Herr Faber stopped visiting, but I remember thinking that, surely now, Matthias would be happier. I imagined him talking to me about the trip he was planning, and for a while we did just that, turning glossy pages of travel books as we pronounced names of foreign cities and mountains. Yet, I felt a new formality between us and didn't know how to change things back to the way they had been.

Perhaps Matthias already knew what I wouldn't understand until much later, that he wouldn't see any of those cities and mountains which I would explore as an adult— not because they could never match the stories he had told me about them—but because to visit them would have broken the order of punishment he had chosen for himself.

We sat at his table one late afternoon, turning the pages of a book with photos of Ireland, when someone knocked. Matthias glanced at me, then jumped up to open the door. The man who came in was tall and had wide hands that carried a bottle of red wine.

"I want to spend some time with my friend now, Hanna," Matthias said without looking at me.

I turned a page of the Ireland book, then another. "What's your name?" I stared at the man.

"Hanna." Matthias laid one hand on my shoulder. "You can come back tomorrow."

I darted one last glance at the man, a warning, I hoped, but I don't think it changed anything. Within the next few weeks, the man took up a pattern of seeing Matthias on Mondays and Thursdays, leaving the mark of his visits on Matthias's body as if Matthias felt so flawed that he had to search for someone to confirm it.

✍ Floating in My Mother's Palm

My mother liked to swim during thunderstorms. Ignoring our housekeeper's warnings, she'd set out for the old quarry hole at the end of our street, her bathing suit under a loose shift, her legs bare. She'd fold her shift and hang it across a branch of one of the birches that crowded each other along the edge of the quarry. While the summer air cooled off with rain, the water in the quarry hole seemed to heat up around her, mysterious bubbles like quicksilver stirred by the movement of her long arms and legs.

At home Frau Brocker would hide a sharp knife under the tablecloth to cut the lightning before it could strike the quarry or our house. While thunder cracked across the sky, she'd sit with her hands folded, whispering prayers of fear to the Virgin Mary.

She carried so many fears that my mother didn't have: fear of the dark, of moths, storms, and deep water, fears I too felt immune to, fears that led Frau Brocker into superstitious rituals which my mother asked me to respect.

"It's her way," she said. "She needs to do those things."

My mother swims in churning water, her face damp from cool drops that descend upon her as if magnetized by the quarry hole. Wet now, her long blond hair looks dark. Her legs kick the water into frothing swirls which she leaves behind. She dives—a long smooth shape—arching her back underwater before her head and shoulders emerge above the surface like a reed springing back into place.

My mother was taller than most of the other women in Burgdorf, and she wore her blond hair loose across her shoulders instead of taming it into a permanent or bun. She walked the way she swam—with long, easy movements.

I grew up watching her paint. Her easel used to stand in our living room, and I played around her feet while she worked. But when I was five, she hired Frau Brocker to take care of me and our apartment, while she claimed a cluster of rooms on the third floor and hired Siegfried Tegern to design a studio for her. He brought two carpenters who tore down the walls and replaced most of the facade with a sheet of glass.

For weeks after they were finished, a fine plaster dust continued to drift through the staircase, settling in my throat until I felt as if I were swallowing through a layer of cotton. I wasn't even allowed inside my mother's studio unless I knocked at the door. Hands behind my back, I'd stalk around, looking at the canvases stacked against the walls, breathing in the familiar, lost scent of oil paint.

At first people stopped on the sidewalk, staring up; they hadn't seen a window that size, except in department stores. Perhaps they believed that, by secluding herself in a place above them, my mother considered herself better than they. Or maybe their uneasiness came from the fear that my mother would expose too much of them. The window was up so high that none of them could look through

it. Even from the upper floors of the houses across the
street, it was impossible to see my mother inside her studio.

Here, surrounded by light, she painted the town which
fascinated and confined her, always more brilliant in color
than in reality, as if she wanted to force it into the shape of
the vision she carried within.

*Lightning divides the sky like a new scar, and my mother raises
her face toward the cool drops that fall faster now, harder. She can
dance in the water without her feet touching the ground. She does
this by twirling her arms in such a way that her body propels itself
around. One early summer evening, when I'm nine, she shows me
how. My father is at a dentists' convention in Bremen, and Frau
Brocker has left for the day. My mother and I walk to the quarry
hole, shed the dresses we wear above our bathing suits, and run
into the water as raindrops strike our bare shoulders. The water is
warmer than the air, and I feel giddy and daring as I race my
mother toward the middle.*

When my mother was a girl, trucks would come to the
quarry empty and leave filled with gravel which huge
cranes dredged from the hole that grew wider and deeper
with each month. But one day water bubbled up from the
bottom, and gradually the hole filled with water as if trying
to replenish itself with the core it had been robbed of. It
didn't take long for the children in Burgdorf to discover the
quarry as a swimming hole. They leapt off the edges; some
tied ropes to the sturdier trees, swung themselves over the
water, and dropped with shrieks.

*Luminous bubbles form around my arms, my legs, and when we
reach a place too deep for us to stand, my mother teaches me how
to dance. She twirls around, and I try to imitate her movements.*

At first I'm clumsy, slow, but soon I find that I, too, can dance in the storm, alone, without holding onto her. When we leave the quarry hole, the brilliant lights have stopped flashing across the sky, and the only sound is that of our sandals slapping against the sidewalk. Though we don't talk about this, neither of us will mention our swim to my father.

One fall the pastor's sister, Hannelore Beier, came to visit my mother and asked if she could look at her paintings. Her crippled, birdlike hands flew toward each canvas in admiration and then they'd halt as if she had to catch them before they could take off on their own. I liked watching those hands which had a peculiar grace of their own. She was our Sunday school teacher, a slight woman who seemed colorless and tired until she read poems to us; then her voice would swell and her hands would draw us into words that were filled with magic and passion, words that held radiance the way my mother's paintings could.

The pastor's sister convinced my mother to exhibit her work at the church fair, and helped her stack the paintings in back of our car. They made eight trips and hung her pictures in the church hall, a dim room in the basement of St. Martin's where Sunday school was usually held and where the bright reds and yellows of my mother's paintings looked even brighter. Though the pastor's sister set up extra lights, they only emphasized the shadows in the corners.

The day of the fair the pastor's sister carried in a soft chair from the rectory; my mother sat at one end of the hall, her blond hair brushed back from her forehead, wearing her purple dress. Neighbors who'd wondered for years what my mother was painting came and stared at the pictures. "But the colors aren't right," they whispered to each other and the pastor's sister raised her hands as if to quiet them. I wanted to kick their shins, trip them on their way to the stairs, but my mother smiled as if this was just what she had hoped to achieve in her work.

I'm five when my mother teaches me to swim. She ties my red ball into her shopping net; the sisal feels rough against my fingers when it is dry, but once we take the ball into the quarry hole, the fibers become wet, sleek. Big boys dive from the rocks at the other end of the quarry. Their shouts echo, and when their bodies hit the surface, columns of silver splash across the sky. I hold on to the net. One of my mother's hands supports my belly.

Sometimes my mother was far away from me though she was in the same room, as if she were still painting inside her mind, guiding her brush across an imaginary canvas. Although I knew that, soon, I'd have her with me again in those intermittent flashes of intensity which she directed toward me, it wasn't enough.

One day, when she seemed to have forgotten that I sat waiting for her in the corner of her studio, I imagined myself lighting a match and raising it to the painting she was working on. I could see the flames race across the canvas, spread to the pictures stacked against the wall, curl their edges, black—I hid my face in my hands. What was wrong with me? I loved my mother's paintings, loved most of them better than the actual places. Yet, I would have set fire to her studio if it had meant she would belong to me from then on. What kept me from destroying her work, I believe, was the certainty that it would crush an integral part of her, a part that could not be healed.

As an adult I would return to Burgdorf and find a stack of my mother's pictures which my father stored in the attic after her death. Two of her paintings I took back with me to hang inside my house. One is of the Rhein at *Hochwasser*, high water: floods swirl across the meadow between the river's bed and the dike, uprooting unsteady trees and cleansing the winter's debris from the meadows and clumps of trees. The other painting shows the quarry hole during a storm, the somber sky highlighted by streaks of silver that make the water look as if it were bubbling. If I look closely, I can almost see myself floating in my mother's palm. Yet, when I shut my eyes, I find a different image of my mother releasing me as we dance in the storm and twirl in separate circles that cause the water to ripple from us in widening rings which merge in one ebbing bracelet of waves where the borders of the quarry meet the water, far from the center where my mother and I continue to spin our bodies in the radiant sheen of lightning.

✐ Dogs of Fear

Siegfried Tegern's seven dogs tore him apart one sweltering summer evening in a meadow between the Rhein and the dike. We'd become accustomed to seeing him walk through Burgdorf, gripping a leash that fanned into seven strands like a whip with so many tails; they coiled themselves into the collars of his dogs as they pulled ahead of him, controlled by his commands. He was an architect, a tall man with gray hair and smooth skin, who wore a suit even when he trained his dogs. He and his wife, Angelika, kept themselves separate from the people in Burgdorf. Newcomers to the town nine years before, they'd built a stucco house with a solarium near the Rhein.

"It was his dream that started it," Angelika Tegern told Herr Pastor Beier after the police had shot her husband's seven dogs. The pastor's sister—since it was not told in the confessional but in the pastor's living room—repeated the story to Frau Brocker, who rushed to the pay-library to be the first to bestow the news upon Trudi Montag. From then on it became knowledge we all shared, knowledge that made us bolt up in our beds late at night and grasp the sheets against our shoulders when, from a distance, the howling of a dog drifted through our open windows.

Sometimes we saw Angelika Tegern walk along the top of the dike as if retracing the steps her husband had taken, and when she came to that meadow she'd stop, standing motionless, her chin raised toward the gray shifting bands of waves as though, in the stretch of high grass between the dike and the river, she saw the seven dogs gathering around her husband in one last ritual dance.

"It was his dream," Angelika Tegern told the pastor. "Not just one dream—they came rather frequently, all of them alike. In the dream Siegfried died. He could feel it each time, not the pain, but the sense of powerlessness. He'd wake, screaming, his hands flying to his face, his chest, as he wiped away the blood he believed he was covered with."

Siegfried didn't know why. Didn't know how. Except that his death would be violent, and that he was unable to avert it. In the dream he stood in a meadow between the dike and the river. Not the meadow he saw when he climbed the dike near his house, but the meadow he'd never been to. The path, which ran from the dike to the river, was unfamiliar to him; yet, he could describe it in detail to his wife when he woke up shaking with the certainty of his death. The path angled to the left where four poplars leaned into each other although no other trees grew close to them; a flat rock lay embedded in the grass just before the path branched into the trail that ran parallel to the Rhein.

To protect himself, Siegfried Tegern bought a guard dog, a German shepherd that he walked every evening, staying away from the Rhein, though he and Angelika had chosen the land for their house because it was close to the river. When the dreams wouldn't cease, he bought six more German shepherds within the next few months. Still, he'd wake up during the night, his body sweating with fear, and find his wife's arms around him as she held him in his trembling until he'd reassured himself that he was safe. His skin took on the texture of creased paper; under his eyes it gathered itself into bruised pouches.

The rose hedges around their house were torn out and replaced by a high metal fence. Siegfried took time off from work to train his dogs in obedience. "They'll protect both of us," he told his wife. To give them added strength, he fed them chunks of beef lung once a week. Anton Immers saved them for him in the back room of his butcher shop, and Siegfried would boil them early on Saturday mornings when Angelika was still asleep. He'd open the windows to let out the gray steam that rose above the pink froth on the surface of the boiling water; yet, when Angelika came downstairs for her first cup of coffee, she'd feel herself enveloped by a sweet, dank smell as if something were about to rot. She tried to convince herself that the dogs were good for Siegfried, although they urinated on her rhododendrons, destroyed the beds of impatiens she'd planted around the patio, and circled the house that lay like a sanctuary within the fence her husband had built. When people walked by, the dogs barked and threw themselves against the chain links that vibrated in a metallic chant long after the sidewalk was empty.

Gradually, Siegfried's control over them increased. When he led them along the sidewalks of our town, they'd walk ahead of him without becoming entangled. One Saturday morning we saw them in the open market; they sat quietly with Siegfried while he compared the prices on the slates the farmers had stuck in their crates of fruits and vegetables. Since it was late in the morning, most had crossed out the original amounts and scribbled lower prices underneath. Siegfried bought two pounds of peaches from Frau Braunmeier and one head of red cabbage from Herr Neumann. After he paid, he whispered something to his dogs, and they got up like one huge animal, one mass of fur and muscles.

"I don't know when he decided to find the meadow from his dream," Angelika Tegern told the pastor and his sister, who was already preserving the words in her mind, molding them into the story she would tell Frau Brocker. She would start out by talking about fear, the architect's fear that did not stop after he purchased the dogs, the fear that even took hold of his wife and which the pastor's sister could see in her face after his death, when she sat stiffly in the leather chair of the pastor's living room. The arthritic hands of the pastor's sister, which had drawn themselves toward her palms and looked like the claws of a large bird, would weave the words into a tapestry as bright and rich as the pictures the dentist's wife painted of the town.

Angelika Tegern told the pastor: "He believed the dreams would stop if he went there. 'The dogs will be with me,' he said, as if that made a difference, and when I told him he didn't even know if the meadow was real, his answer was that it had to be."

So convinced was he of its existence, that early every evening, he'd set out for longer walks with his dogs, first searching the river north in the direction of Oberhausen, then south toward Düsseldorf. Water swirled white around the edges of the jetties as if someone had poured soap into it, and the current seemed to move in opposite directions. Like pesky insects, motorboats and kayaks flitted in and out between the freighters. Branches and debris drifted in the river. Once he saw the body of a yellow cat bobbing in the waves, back up and legs down. He couldn't see its head.

He came to know the changing shoreline: sandy crescents, walls secured with mortar, pebbled stretches of beach, meadows that were lush and green after a heavy rain. In Düsseldorf the embankment was built in three segments: first a mound of boulders that rose two meters above the river's surface; then a flat walkway; and above it a cemented slant of stones that stretched itself at least ten meters to the sidewalk and street. In Oberkassel a straight sandy beach was bordered by a wide meadow where, every fall, the biggest circus in the area set up its tents.

Some evenings he walked until it was too dark to see, and he'd come home too tired to hang up the leash he'd made, a leather loop with a metal ring to which seven leashes were fastened. Inside the fence, his dogs stumbled into one knot of limbs and snouts, dropping into sleep that was only interrupted by the involuntary twitching of some leg or tail as if a great beast were rehearsing the vaguely remembered details of an ancient hunt.

Siegfried lay awake, dreading the dream that would certainly suck him into the familiar terror. Through the window a narrow shaft of dull light seeped from the moon and touched his forehead like a priest administering last rites. Shivering, he closed his eyes, but it was as though the moon had coated the lining of his eyelids with a mirror that reflected his dream.

But one Saturday in May he came up the dike with the sun behind him, and as his body met his long shadow at the crest in a tight shape before disengaging itself, he recognized the landscape of his dream: the angle of the path as it rolled down the other side of the dike and through the meadow; the clump of poplars that rose above the wildflowers; the flat rock that lay embedded in the ground where the path led into the trail which traced the edge of the Rhein. And—just as he had known it would be—he felt drained of all fear. All he felt was a lightness, joy almost, as he stood there on the dike, watching the river, which was heavy with rain and melted snow from the mountains in the south. It ran high and fast, flooding the tips of the jetties and tossing its gray waves against the embankment. Parallel to the steps leading up the dike was a yellow strip of metal with arrows to indicate the levels of past floods.

The dogs gathered themselves around his legs, and he let his hands glide over their smooth amber and black heads. From the river came the sound of a barge. Its rusting hull strained against the current. Canvas sheets fastened with ropes covered the cargo, and a lifeboat lay stored upside down on top of the canvas. The German flag—black, gold and red—fluttered from its stern. *Eugenie, Bremen* proclaimed the white letters on the side.

Siegfried walked down to the wide stretch of grassland that was bordered by the dike and the river. It was dotted with buttercups and cornflowers and patches of heather that gave off the hazy scent of spring. Above the treeline across the river rose an airplane like a luminous bird, immense and weightless. A boat with two white sails crisscrossed from one bank of the river to the other.

"That night the dream did not take hold of him," Angelika Tegern told the pastor, and the pastor's sister laid one of her crippled hands on the shoulder of the architect's wife, trying to protect her from something too late to prevent. "He came home tired but calm. And between us it was almost the way it had been before the dreams. He woke rested the next morning, convinced he'd found a way to stop the dream. Perhaps if he had left it at that. . . . But he wanted to go back. Needed to go back, though I asked him not to."

Sunday morning Siegfried took the dogs back to the meadow and let them run free. Wind rippled their thick fur as they chased each other in playful circles. When the sun moved from behind a cloud and warmed the moist air, Siegfried folded his suit jacket to make a pillow for himself to sit on, stretched out his legs, and leaned his back against the damp bark of a poplar. Out on the river, the hotel ship *Zürich* floated by, music drifting from its decks. White ribbons of water spurted from its stern and from an opening in its side. The sun was strong, comforting, and he half closed his eyes as the dogs settled down close to him. He stroked their sunwarmed backs; when he stopped, they nuzzled his palms and he laughed and reached for them again.

In the bright sunlight that made everything seem as if it were filtered through a stretched piece of gauze, he searched for sticks which he tossed for his dogs to fetch; their noses quivered as their eyes followed the wide arc of the sticks; yet, they waited until he nodded his consent before they darted after them, and when they brought them back, they laid them at his feet like offerings.

The meadow was nearly two kilometers from the house, and he made it a habit to take his dogs there after work. He walked them along the top of the dike until he reached the path, and then he descended and crossed the meadow to the trail by the river. During June the swollen body of the Rhein receded. Beer stands opened along the river; hikers and bicyclers stopped for a quick glass or two before disappearing into the clumps of bushes along the path, buttoning their pants as they emerged.

By July the Rhein was back in its normal bed, though the watermarks left by the flood still crusted the boulders of the jetties and the embankment. From a distance, the water was the color of dark moss, but when he walked closer, it became a shimmering blend of brown and green. Siegfried Tegern's skin lost its bruised look as he came to trust nights that would carry him into mornings without the old dream of fear. He smiled when he walked his dogs through town. One day he tied them to the bicycle stand outside the town hall while he went inside to check on a deed. The dogs sat erect, snouts raised toward the bell tower, and howled, an eerie sound that entered the arched windows of the town hall and flooded the surrounding streets.

That evening he returned to the meadow and sat under the poplars while his dogs played in the knee-high grass. White fluff sifted from the branches of the poplars like angel's hair: it settled on his shoulders, his sleeves, and sometimes he caught a downy tuft when the breeze bore it gently past his hands. It was almost the color of sheep's wool but not nearly as heavy and dense; tangled within the soft clusters were dried pods and brittle twigs.

Resting his back against one of the trunks, it occurred to him how fortunate he was to have rid himself of the fear. He remembered what it had been like before he discovered the meadow, but suddenly the meadow was just as it appeared in the dream; yet, this time he saw more: himself, standing by the poplars, arms angled as if fending off an attacker, and he saw his dogs, not playing, but advancing toward him, crouching as though preparing to leap. His old fear rose in one hot bolt, and two of the dogs jerked up their heads as if some scent in the air had caught their attention.

And as the fear of his dreams seized upon him—that familiar sweat fear of death—stronger than ever before, it drew the dogs closer to him. Cautiously they sniffed, their broad noses nuzzling his legs, his hands, and when he stood up and pushed them away, they backed off, as though confused. The hair on their black and amber backs rose ever so slightly, and they panted, flecks of spittle on their tongues. One of them, the bravest one certainly, let out a slow growl from deep within its throat and heaved itself forward, teeth closing around the bottom of Siegfried's trousers. Though he shouted his commands, the other dogs jumped at him too. He tried to ward them off with his feet and his elbows as they crowded around him, low, some leaping, until one of them drew a trace of blood from a small gash in his throat. And as he cried out in protest, the dogs thrust themselves into a frenzy of greed that blotted out all memory of commands obeyed.

After the police shot the seven dogs, we asked ourselves if, by buying the dogs, Siegfried Tegern had brought on his death himself. We told each other he could have avoided it so easily. And yet, there were times—especially late at night when we were startled by the sounds of a restless dog —that we couldn't feel all that sure anymore and almost believed his death had been waiting for him in that meadow all along.

The Thread of His Grieving

O nce I was almost caught stealing flowers for my brother's grave. I'd done it before, making sure to check the paths of the Burgdorf cemetery before I took flowers from other graves, but I never took more than one. I'd gather them in my hands until Joachim got a bigger bouquet than anyone else, and I'd try to feel the sadness I read about in our housekeeper's romances.

In those books there was always the single tear that slid down the heroine's cheek without blemishing her complexion or dignity. I can still see myself at twelve, trying to squeeze out that one significant tear. But I simply wasn't skilled at producing tears; I cried too seldom, and the few times I did, it was in wet, noisy gulps of frustration over something Rolf had said or done. Most of our battles were over his mother's attention, which I had to reclaim every day and he took home with him at night.

How I yearned for real tragedy. But the most tragic thing in my life—my brother's death—had happened when I was two, and I couldn't even remember his face, or touching him. He was just a sequence of letters on the family headstone below the names of my mother's parents;

still, he was my only link to real tragedy, and I kept returning to the cemetery, trying to feel his loss.

I badgered my parents with questions about his death, and I took their words and filled in the spaces until I could evoke the afternoon he'd died and watch it on an inner screen like a film I could rewind or stop at will. Since we had no photos of Joachim, his features kept changing for me, but he always had reddish hair like my father.

My mother rocked my brother for three hours after he died. He was only nine days old. Sitting on a wooden chair inside the hospital room, she held him in her arms, rocking her upper body back and forth though her chair stayed motionless. It was as though the nuns' prophecy about her pregnancy with me had suddenly caught up with her.

At first my father tried to have her relinquish the dead infant to the nurse who spoke to my mother in soothing words. He felt powerless as she sat there, staring straight ahead, her body rigid, their child in her arms, rocking. Rocking. Finally, allowing his grief to match hers, my father knelt beside her, his arms around her and his son, his body a shadow of her rocking motion.

And so my mother sat there for hours, her arms around my brother, encircled by my father's arms. From time to time the doctor entered the room, and my father told him, "Not yet." By now he felt the soothing rocking himself, felt the thread of his grieving woven into that of my mother's.

The muted light of the winter afternoon gave way to dusk that stripped the white from the walls and made all sounds in the street seem to come from far away. My father laid one finger against the cheek of his child. Only a few hours earlier his son was still breathing, a sound as if he were blowing bubbles from a place deep within his narrow chest. His face was flushed, but slowly it turned ashen. Though his cheeks stayed red for a while, they soon faded until his skin became translucent and his lips took on a bluish tinge. And his rattly breathing—it made the room seem small and opened up a wish in my father, the wish for it to end, the wish to spare Joachim the struggle as his lungs filled with fluid.

Gradually my mother's body lost some of the rigidity that first made her cling to the child while others tried to take him from her. My father knew she'd be able to let go —not yet, though—but with each moment it seemed more possible. He knew this child, knew the way his hands had formed fists, then released themselves into curled fingers as he nursed. He knew the way his son's eyes had resisted closing when he fell asleep as if he sensed how brief his life would be and felt reluctant to miss one single moment.

And what my father had to do now was know his son in this new, silent form. Remember his changed face, longer somehow and solemn, his still hands. Remember him like this to carry himself and my mother through mourning.

The day I almost got caught stealing flowers for Joachim, I took the vase with the sharp point at its bottom from behind our headstone and walked over to the nearest faucet. All of the graves were covered with flowers and bushes. Impatiens and geraniums, fuchsias and rhododendrons, lilies and roses thickened the air with a lavish scent that slowed down the wing beats of the birds that lived in the cemetery. Noisy and secure, hundreds of them perched on headstones and nested in the lush hedges as if they knew that this was a safe place where cats and children wouldn't chase them. Often I heard them long before I reached the gate, long before the familiar scent reached for me.

On several graves were lanterns with short, thick candles. Headstones listed the names of people in the order in which they'd died, most of them old, some of them children who had died too young. Like Joachim. Whose name was the last on our headstone.

Frau Weskopp stood at the faucet in her black coat, holding her watering can beneath the spout. It was easy to tell who the widows were: they spent many hours at the cemetery, tending the family graves; they wore black for many years; they arrived on their bicycles with watering cans hanging from their handlebars; they wore thick nylons and shoes with stocky heels; they carried rolled-up umbrellas in case it rained; they sat on benches with other widows, talking while gazing over the rows of graves.

Frau Weskopp turned off the faucet and stepped aside. Deep lines ran across her cheeks and forehead. She had the face of someone who knew how to grieve. "Visiting your brother?" she asked.

I nodded and filled our vase with water.

She glanced up toward the scattered clouds. "Better not stay too long. We may get a storm this afternoon."

At least three times she had told me how lucky my brother was that Herr Pastor Beier had christened him so soon after he was born. "Otherwise he'd be in purgatory."

Her husband and both sons had fought on the Russian front and had died the same year. Their names were engraved not only on the headstone but also in the last column of the tall war monument at the entrance to the cemetery.

As I knelt on my brother's grave and wedged the sharp point of the vase into the dirt, I imagined my mother holding Joachim, imagined her as I had so often, my father holding both of them, rocking, my brother wrapped in a white blanket that covered him from his feet to his shoulders, his head lying securely in the bend of my mother's left arm, her right hand resting on his chest.

I got my eyes to fill with tears by letting them go out of focus and staring straight ahead until they burned, but when I tried to blink out a tear, my eyes dried right away.

Except for the birds, it was quiet in the cemetery. I sat back on my heels and wiped my hands on my skirt. On my thumb was a cut; I pressed against it, but even that didn't bring on tears. The cut was from stealing garden doors. Stealing wasn't actually the right word. Late the night before, I'd sneaked out to meet Rolf Brocker and Karin Baum. The three of us had started out behind Anton Immers's house, and whenever we got to a garden door, we'd lift it from its hinges and drag it around the next corner, where we'd leave it leaning against a tree or fence. Some of those gates were heavy; one of them fell on Karin's foot and another cut my thumb, but the three of us managed to carry them. This morning people all over Burgdorf had been searching for their garden doors.

I brushed the dirt from my bare knees and walked to where our lane intersected with the main path. No one was there. The air was moist, warm. A bouquet of daisies stood next to the headstone of Trudi Montag's father. I pulled a daisy from the blue jar and walked to the next grave. A rose . . . a snapdragon . . . a carnation . . . The vase on the Weskopp's grave was filled with violets, and I took one of them, deep purple with black markings along the tips of the petals. By now Joachim's bouquet had flowers of just about every color, and I carried it back to his grave. Sitting on the edge of the stone, I arranged the flowers so that the tallest ones were in the center.

"That's a pretty bouquet, Hanna."

My head snapped up.

Frau Weskopp was standing behind me. "Especially that violet." Her lips closed into a tight line.

I felt as if the flowers bore tags with the names of the dead. "Thank you," I managed to say.

"Where did you get them?"

"Home," I said quickly before something within me made me confess.

That's what she seemed to be waiting for—a confession. But I kept silent, though my heart was racing. The deep creases on her forehead pressed the flesh between them into puffy welts. Finally she turned away and walked down the path toward the exit.

I pushed the vase deeper into the earth. That's where Joachim was. What was left of him. We'd never unhinge garden doors together and hide them around the corner. We'd never swim in the Rhein together or ride our bikes or play ball or—I caught my arms against my stomach, tight. Rocked myself back and forth. All at once I saw Joachim and myself, sitting on my wooden sled on top of the dike, our faces red from the cold. *"Hold on!" I shout out to him as I push off. Joachim sits in front of me. My feet are on the metal runners, my arms around my brother's chest. I'm the one holding on; yet, I keep shouting, "Hold on, Joachim!"*

My breath is a white lace scarf that touches his neck and reddish hair. Joachim is almost as tall as I. Sitting straight, I hold on to him as our sled hurtles down a slope that doesn't end. But he is getting smaller in my arms. At first my hands barely meet in front of his jacket, but now I can cross my wrists, then my arms as if I were hugging myself. "Hold on, Joachim," I shout once more, frozen tears on my face. My arms around myself, I know for the first time what it feels like to have lost him, to be without him not only this moment but millions of moments like this, linked and stretching into all my tomorrows. I see myself grown up, my newborn son in my arms, pouring a trickle of holy water over his head, forming the sign of the cross on his forehead, chest, and shoulders, whispering fragile words of insurance against purgatory: "Im Namen des Vaters und des Sohnes und des Heiligen Geistes . . ."

But suddenly my brother is here again, solid in my arms, snow coating his shoulders and swirling around us as the sled races down the white bank. The Rhein is frozen, and as we glide across it, huge turtles and tropical fish swim below the clear ice. On the other side of the river two riders gallop along the bank on blue horses.

Through the Dance of Her Hands

The pastor's sister, Hannelore Beier, was a woman in her thirties with crippled hands. Her fingers overlapped and drew themselves toward her palms, birdlike claws which she refused to hide. When she taught Sunday school, she moved them gracefully, those stiff extensions of herself, weaving the texture of her words into our hearts.

Her eyes looked tired when she quoted passages from the Bible, but she never stayed with the Bible for long. From her bag she'd bring out old books bound in green or red leather; the lines in her face dissolved and her slight body seemed to grow as she took the words of Goethe and Mann and Rilke from the pages of those books and made them breathe as if they were being written now—for us.

Her favorite writer was Rainer Maria Rilke. One winter morning, in the church basement, she read us his poem about the panther in the *Jardin des Plantes, Paris*, and her voice evoked the powerful animal pacing behind the bars of his cage, until to him it seemed as though there were a thousand bars and nothing beyond them. Outside it was snowing wet, thick flakes that fastened themselves like cat tracks to the narrow windows of the church hall before they slid off, leaving watery trails on the glass. We pulled our chairs into a circle that included hers and we barely dared to breathe while she read. We knew what it was like to be that panther. We too felt locked into ourselves at times because we wanted to know everything in the world and were beginning to fear that this would never be possible.

Fräulein Beier copied the poems we liked on lined pages in green ink. Square and awkward, her letters slanted on the left, and when I read them I imagined her stiff fingers setting the tip of the fountain pen against the page, forming those words which opened us to people and places far beyond our town.

She had come to Burgdorf seven years before to keep house for her brother, the pastor of St. Martin's. His old housekeeper, Fräulein Teschner, had turned into a tyrant, restricting his diet, his contact with parishioners of the opposite sex, and the hours he could spend away from the rectory. In despair, he'd called his sister, Hannelore, who was a social worker in Stuttgart. He found a better-paying job for Fräulein Teschner with a surgeon in Düsseldorf, and his sister moved into the rectory. She cooked his enormous meals, ironed his enormous clothes, typed his enormous sermons, and let him schedule his own consultations. She served coffee and gingerbread when he had meetings with young couples who planned to get married.

During Sunday mass she knelt in the front pew of St. Martin's, her face raised to the marble altar, her eyes wide open. Black marble columns supported the arches of the ceiling where her voice rose with others in hymns that collected themselves in echoes and expanded the boundaries of the church. As her voice blazed past the walls, she let herself be lifted by the sounds that streamed through the organ's silver pipes and transformed the silence of the church into a celebration. Yet, when the music faded and the voices receded to murmured prayers, she was drawn back into her isolation.

Every Wednesday morning at seven Hannelore Beier rode her bicycle the two kilometers to the Burgdorf chapel, a white stone building set on a gentle hill near the Sternburg. She entered through the curved door, climbed the stairs to the bell tower, and grasped the rope.

The chapel was built six hundred years ago, and its slate roof was layered like the gray wing feathers of the pigeons that roosted on the tower and the ridge of the steep roof. Their droppings splattered the two benches in front of the chapel. When the pastor's sister rang the bells, they drowned the guttural chorus of the birds, which rose in one swarm, settling in the row of poplars that broke the landscape and cast long shadows across the adjoining wheat fields.

All across town, the old women would mount their bicycles to arrive in time for eight o'clock mass. Their narrow skirts didn't give them much room to move their legs, and so they pedaled slowly while their handbags swung from the handlebars. At the chapel they got off carefully, locked the bicycles, and smoothed their skirts with their palms. Handbags across their left arms, they entered the cool core of the chapel, stopped next to the holy water, then dipped their right forefingers and middle fingers into the basin, and touched their foreheads, bosoms, and shoulders in the familiar sign of the cross.

The side altar held a large statue of the Virgin Mother; there, the women lit candles, closed their eyes, and whispered prayers for the recovery of a relative, the fulfillment of a secret wish, or the relief from eternal punishment for someone who'd died. Their faith in the mercy and power of the Virgin Mary merged with the flames from many other candles, merged and ascended toward, perhaps, a benevolent presence.

Occasionally a man would come to the service or one of the younger women, but most Wednesday mornings the chapel was filled with old women. The rest of the week Herr Pastor Beier read mass at St. Martin's, except for Wednesdays when he climbed on the motor scooter the bishop had assigned to him, and rode to the chapel. Ten minutes before eight he arrived at the side door, his breath in quick gasps, his face red, his black jacket stretched across his huge stomach. In the sacristy, which smelled of incense and damp stone, he struggled into the vestments his sister had laid out for him: first he put on the alb and watched the white linen cover the tops of his black shoes; then he knotted the cincture around his ample waist, kissed the stole before laying it around his neck, and slipped into the chasuble, a long brocade gown with the cross embroidered on the back.

Sometimes, while Herr Pastor Beier raised the sacred chalice, the women heard the scratching of talons against slate high above them, as if the Holy Spirit had chosen to descend upon their ceremony, and they turned their creased faces toward the vaults of the chapel where faint watermarks formed cloudlike designs.

Though they had wrinkles and gray hair, these women didn't think of themselves as old; it was an unspoken fact that each of them carried within, a fact that didn't need to be confirmed because there was always someone who could remember them as girls and recall a half-forgotten detail, someone who—beneath the fine web of lines—still saw the child's face.

They did this for each other, the old women, pulling out the albums of class picnics, of trips to Kaiserswerth and Schloss Burg, pointing to their younger images in fading photographs and whispering to each other: "Remember?" And they continued to do so until they were in their eighties or nineties because, as long as there was someone who had known them as girls, someone who could recollect the quick movements of their limbs, the graceful turn of their smooth necks—they could gaze into their mirrors and see their young reflections.

Most of these women were widows who'd lost their husbands to the war or old age. They lived with one of their children's families and helped with the raising of their grandchildren, with the cooking, the cleaning. They pinched off brown stalks from the geraniums in their window boxes and ironed tablecloths. They knitted sweaters and had their hair set once a week at the beauty parlor. They took care of the family graves. They knew when to interfere and when to remain silent, though they didn't always follow their instincts. They complained bitterly to one another about the size of their rooms, the lack of privacy; yet, they felt sorry for those among them who lived alone.

Most of these women had taken care of their aging parents: entangled between the needs of their parents and the needs of their children, they'd never considered doing otherwise. It had to do with continuity, with responsibility, with the tremendous impact the old had on the young, and as their children grew up and saw their parents take care of their grandparents, they took for granted that, some day, they too would follow that example.

Here in the chapel, while the unyielding wood of the pews pressed against their knees, callused from thousands of masses, the old women felt a timeless connection to one another, a connection that came from celebrating their first communion together and going to the same school even though they might have sat in different classrooms, a connection that came from knowing each other's strengths and weaknesses, from understanding and being a part of each other's stories and histories.

When they left the white chapel, their steps were almost lithe, and they blinked in the morning light. They drifted into circles of four or five, talking among themselves while glancing occasionally at the sky which always changed so quickly: cloud formations moved swiftly with the wind across the sun, causing the temperature to drop or rise in seconds. Even where the sky stayed blue, it was marbled with faint streaks of white. During the summer the poplar seeds with their delicate tufts floated across the fields, clinging to the spears of wheat until the pigeons swooped upon them and carried them away for their nests.

The pastor's sister walked from group to group, greeting the old women who looked upon her with pity. To them she seemed old because they had no early image of her. Flawed like an injured bird, she'd arrived in their town. She had no husband, no children, only her brother, a heavy man nearly twenty years older than she, who'd left home for the seminary by the time she was born and had seen her young only in photos. Her slight figure seemed to recede in the wren-colored dresses she chose for herself. A thin belt pulled the center of her together as if she were about to disappear.

The old women didn't know the power of her voice, which made her entire body come alive when she shared the poems she loved with the children. They didn't know the color in her laugh. They didn't know that sometimes she closed her eyes and imagined herself lying in a summer field of golden-yellow wheat. *The long stalks hide her from anyone who might be looking for her. She breaks off a stalk, runs her fingertips across the end of the stiff spikes at the top of each kernel. She separates one kernel, strips the thin layer of skin that feels like a callus. Underneath is a soft core that tastes like wet flour.*

The young teacher moved to Burgdorf the summer the pastor's sister turned forty. He arrived in the sweltering heat of early August, four weeks before school started, so he could get to know the town. A tall man with blond hair and black eyebrows, he'd grown up in Switzerland, speaking French and German. His name was Lucien Cheronnet, and he had been hired to teach fourth grade at the Catholic school.

The pastor, who was president of the school board, found an apartment for Lucien Cheronnet on the third floor of the white house across from the rectory. His first night there, the young teacher found it impossible to sleep. The heat pressed against his limbs; when he got up from his bed and walked to the open bedroom window, a slight breeze lifted the lace curtain and cooled the sweat on his chest. In the slow light of the moon, the brick gables of the church glowed red as if they contained passions of their own.

That Sunday the pastor invited him to dinner at the rectory with the other members of the school board. While the pastor's sister served them, the young teacher watched her hands fly across the white linen and polished silver with a beauty he'd never believed existed. They were like young birds, those hands, poised to fly off independently, and he wanted to reach out for them, hold them briefly in the cup of his palms before releasing them.

We would have kept her secret had we found her making love with the young teacher down by the river late that summer, but the old women said it was a scandal. They felt angry, betrayed, as if, somehow, the pastor's sister had proven them wrong. Lucien Cheronnet lost his job before starting it, and he called a taxi to take him and Hannelore Beier to the train station in Düsseldorf.

"I wish you'd stay," Herr Pastor Beier told his sister the morning of her departure. He sat across the table from her, his two soft-boiled eggs still covered with knitted egg warmers.

She ate silently.

"I wish I could have acted differently," he said, "but the school board—" He opened his arms in a helpless sweep. "If I can help . . ."

The following Wednesday the bells of the chapel did not
ring, and when the old women arrived—some of them late
or with a button left undone—they found that the pastor's
sister had not come. By the time Sunday mass arrived, it
was evident that she'd left, and we stared at the empty
space in the pew where she used to kneel.

Our new Sunday school teacher, Frau Wilhelmi, read to
us about Moses and his mother, who'd saved the infant's
life by hiding him in a woven basket which she'd smeared
with pitch and slime, then set afloat among the reeds and
water lilies that grew in the shallow water along the river's
edge. But we gazed out of the narrow windows of the
church basement and beyond, imagining the pastor's sister
and the young teacher. *They're on a train that passes through
golden wheat fields and through forests where sunlight turns the
crowns of the trees bright yellow-green and filters into the lower,
darker branches. Hannelore Beier has an open book on her knees
and as she reads poems to the young teacher, she paints the words
for him through the dance of her hands. Lucien Cheronnet captures
her hands in his, lightly, the way one might hold a newly hatched
robin, and brings them to his lips.*

*Their train speeds through cities and crosses rivers until it reaches
Paris. They leave the station, their arms around each other, and
walk to the Jardin des Plantes where the panther paces the length
of his cage. The young teacher nods as Hannelore Beier reaches into
the cage, and strokes the animal's magnificent neck. The panther
arches his back. A curtain lifts from his pupils as the pastor's sister
slides aside the bolt that has kept him in captivity. His eyes like
sudden, green flames, he recognizes a world beyond the bars of his
cage.*

✐ Of Weaker Stock

One of the regulars at Trudi Montag's pay-library was Anton Immers, the retired butcher, who liked to read nurse-and-doctor novels. Perhaps descriptions of operating rooms recalled for him the days when he'd drawn a knife swiftly through pulsing flesh. His granddaughter, Sybille Immers, was in my class, the only girl taller than I.

One Saturday afternoon as he shuffled out of the pay-library with two novels under his arm, Trudi Montag whispered to me that he was a three-months baby.

"What do you mean?" It was hard to imagine the old man as an infant.

"Child—" She shook her head as if exasperated by my naïveté. "His parents were married three months before he was born."

"You mean—they did it before they got married?"

Trudi Montag nodded. Smiled.

"How do you know?"

"I looked it up in the town registry," she said, and I wondered what else she'd found in the ancient town records that were kept in the basement of the *Rathaus*, the town hall with a bell tower and arched windows whose curved tops were inlaid with blue bricks.

Anton Immers bred violets on the windowsill and shelves of the room he occupied on the second floor of his son's house. His daughter-in-law, Irmtraud, complained about the smell of the plant food which the old man concocted from secret ingredients. The mixture, which stood in a pail next to her washing machine, smelled suspiciously close to cow dung and rotting fish, yet became odorless as soon as he worked it into the soil.

His violets ranged from deep purple to pale pink. Their blossoms were huge, their leaves a lush green. Anton Immers had passed on the butcher shop to his son, Anton, just as he had passed on his name and his house, but he still kept financial control of the family; his daughter-in-law had to come to him for extra expenses, enduring the humiliation of having him refuse her money to repair her outmoded sewing machine and buy material for the matching winter coats she wanted to sew for herself and her daughter, Sybille.

Every morning he dressed in a dark suit and watered his hundreds of plants while listening to Wagner records. His coarse hands, which had slaughtered cattle and pigs, tenderly nipped off dying leaves and blossoms, and transplanted seedlings into clay pots filled with rich soil. The flowers' perfection gave him more pleasure than anything else had ever given him. Other people in Burgdorf, who grew violets and spent more time on their plants than he, didn't have nearly the same success. They suspected the fertilizer had little to do with the profuse growth of the retired butcher's plants. They suspected Anton Immers's violets grew so well because they were afraid.

If a plant failed to thrive, he'd set it on the ledge outside his window where he'd let it shrivel in the cold air while the elite plants had to witness its slow death. During the summer, a night in the shop's meat locker would bring the same results. In winter, when he brought in the plant, he sometimes had to brush snow from its brittle leaves before he placed it on the table next to his bed as an example to the others. There it would stay for weeks, turning brown and dry, until he decided it was time to annihilate the next plant. Carefully he'd choose the weakest one, feeling the other plants recoil.

"This can happen to you too if you don't grow," the butcher's father murmured to his plants in the mornings when he rotated them a quarter turn so that each part of their foliage received equal amounts of light. "This can happen to you too."

As a young man, Anton Immers had broken his back while slaughtering a cow; though it had healed eventually, he'd been left with a constant ache in the lower region of his spine, more like stiffness than anything else. But he hadn't retired from the butcher shop until five years earlier when he turned seventy-seven. Since then he'd been growing violets and winning the annual competition at St. Martin's Church for the best violets. The winner's plants decorated the nativity scene in the wing of the church all through December until Epiphany on January 6. Surrounded by Anton Immers's prime violets knelt life-size, carved statues of the Virgin Mother and Saint Josef; between them the Christ Child lay in his manger on real straw, raising one hand in divine benediction. Rows of candles, which the people of Burgdorf would light for their prayers, separated the Holy Family from the pews.

"It's not right," the old women, whose flowers used to win the award, told Herr Pastor Beier. "It's not right to let a plant killer display his violets in the nativity scene."

. . .

In the small brick house that used to be his, Anton Immers kept to his room except for meals, listening to Wagner's *Niebelungenring* and *Lohengrin*, his view restricted to what he could see through the panes of his window that faced Schlosserstrasse. Across the street was Potter's, a long, narrow bar with tables in the back. Some of the men, who got there as soon as it opened, had gone to school and been in the war with Anton Immers. He'd watch them enter the dim bar and, late in the afternoon, stumble out, blinking in the fading light.

One of them, Kurt Heidenreich, arrived every morning at nine-forty on his bicycle in beige trousers and a gray cardigan. It pained Anton Immers to watch a man two years younger take five minutes to dismount from his bicycle; yet, at the same time he felt a familiar sense of superiority as Kurt Heidenreich locked his bike, wobbled to the bolted door, and tried the handle. Muttering to himself, he'd step back from the door, head tilted, and stand on the sidewalk, staring at the bar. After a few minutes he'd move forward again, rattling the door handle. This happened every day until Herr Potter, who owned the bar, opened at ten.

On Tuesdays the bar was closed; yet, Kurt Heidenreich would be there as always, awkwardly getting off his bicycle and repeating his ritual. Until ten-thirty he'd stand in front of the locked door, shaking his head and mumbling. Finally he'd mount his bike once more and pedal the five blocks to his daughter's house where he had a large room with a washbasin and a radio.

What a fool, Anton Immers thought as he watched him, what a fool. He straightened the lapel of his suit jacket. Kurt Heidenreich had been one of the popular boys in school. But he turned out to be of weaker stock. Like some of the violets.

· · ·

One Wednesday morning in summer Anton Immers woke to the sound of the chapel bells as usual, and knew if he glanced outside, he'd see the old women on their bicycles heading for mass. But there was another sound—something scratching against the side of his house. When he climbed out of bed and peered through the window, Albert Zimmermann, the painter, was standing on a ladder that leaned against the house, a bucket of paint in one hand.

"What's going on?" He stuck out his gray head.

"Good morning, Herr Immers. Your son hired me to paint the trim."

"News to me."

He watched every brush stroke. At first the painter tried to talk with him, but soon he became irritated as the old man found fault with almost everything he did.

"Close your window, please, so I can paint the trim," the painter finally said.

"Be careful you don't get any on the glass," Anton Immers warned before he retreated inside. His face pressed against the pane, he slid it up and down as his eyes followed the motion of the paintbrush.

The painter thought it was funny the way the wrinkled face crushed itself against the glass like elephant skin as if to block his view of the room, but when the butcher mouthed words and jabbed fingers in the direction of spots he had missed, the painter aimed his brush toward the window. Anton Immers's mouth opened in a howl, but by then the painter was too agitated to stop himself and painted across it—the old face behind the glass—painted it over with Eggshell #23, square by square, until all he could see was the sheen of the off-white paint. He heard the wailing from inside the house, heard the old man's fists pounding against the glass, and steadied his ladder against the wall.

When Irmtraud Immers dragged her husband's father from the blind window that wouldn't yield his reflection any longer, she pulled back his wrists so he couldn't heave his fists through the glass and held him until he crumpled in her arms. She helped him to his bed and lowered him onto the mattress. The room was filtered with an opaque light that made the blossoms of the violets look heavy and cast a damp pallor on the old man's features.

The daughter-in-law shivered at the sudden image of his coffin being lowered into the dark earth, at the pastor sprinkling holy water and making the sign of the cross above the final mound of earth. "Rest now," she whispered to the old man who stared past her, his breathing fast and shallow. "Rest." But already she was glancing around the room, choosing the wall where she would set up her modern sewing machine and a long table on which she'd cut heavy blue wool for her and her daughter's coats.

In the kitchen she filled a metal pail with soapy water and, without saying a word, brought it out to the painter who stood at the base of his ladder, a flustered expression on his face.

"I'm sorry," he mumbled. "I don't know why . . . I really am."

He climbed back up the ladder with the pail and washed the paint from the window. As the room emerged through the white smears, he first noticed the dresser with the record player and, above it, a framed portrait of the old man in uniform. And then he saw Anton Immers lying on the bed in his suit, surrounded by hundreds of plants, like someone laid out for his funeral.

But Anton Immers did not die until early that December, his body smaller somehow, shrunken, and when the painter entered St. Martin's Church for the service and saw the coffin among rows of violets which the old women of Burgdorf had brought, he felt a shock of recognition. It was only a week after Frau Weskopp had won first prize for her violets and the right to exhibit them in the nativity scene. Anton Immers had refused to enter the competition. Some of the people in town thought that the brief time without light last summer had drained him of his strength, but the old women suspected that his violets had ranked him inferior and—in a bizarre reversal of his own ritual—had let him shrivel to death.

A Crime of Passion

In the spring of 1958 Eva Starmen and Werner Bilder were killed while making love in his car behind the gym of the Catholic school. Someone shot them: Werner twice in the back of his neck, Eva several times into her chest and abdomen.

"He must have sneaked up on them," Frau Brocker said when she described the deaths to me and Renate. "Probably shot the man from behind while the woman had to watch." She shuddered, her eyes glistening and dark as if she could see the scene of the murder. "It was a crime of passion."

Frau Brocker knew all about passion: she had an illegitimate son because she'd danced with an American soldier at the end of the war.

During that summer, two more couples were killed the same way. Renate and I didn't know them, but we saved the pictures the Burgdorf newspaper had published, first showing the live victims, then the cars in which they had been killed. According to the articles, the police suspected

Hans-Jürgen Braunmeier, an escaped murderer, whose parents owned the dairy farm near the Rhein. As a boy, Hans-Jürgen had swung kittens by their tails, spinning them as fast as he could before releasing them to smash against the walls of the barn and slide off, stunned piles of bones and skin. This information came from one of his old classmates who, according to the newspaper, had witnessed Hans-Jürgen burning a tomcat's front paws when he was seven years old.

One day after school Renate and I spotted his father in the pay-library, checking out westerns. With his thin shoulder blades and tired eyes, he didn't look like the father of a murderer, but Trudi Montag assured us that he was not as blameless as he seemed. "Things go on in that family—" Her voice drew itself into a hush. "I'd be ashamed to tell you." But she refused to say more.

We bought strands of licorice at Becker's grocery store next door and ate them as we walked to the end of Schreberstrasse where a huge willow stood above the narrow brook. Grabbing a fistful of thin branches, Renate swung herself across the creek. When her feet reached the other side, she stumbled on her short leg and let go of the branches. I caught them as they swung back to me, pushed myself off, and flew across the brook. I dropped down next to her, and we sat cross-legged on the tufts of grass that covered both banks of the brook.

"You think Trudi Montag knows more about the murderer?" The gums around Renate's front teeth looked black from the licorice. She picked up a stick and fished a leaf out of the water. In the damp air her black hair was even frizzier than usual.

I shook my head. "She would tell," I said. "She always does."

By the time we'd walked back to my house, we'd convinced ourselves that Trudi Montag, indeed, didn't know anything beyond what the newspaper had written about the murders and the torturing of the cats.

When Renate and I pressed Frau Brocker for more details about Hans-Jürgen Braunmeier, she told us, "About ten years ago he killed his financée. And the man she was with. In a car. You two were little kids when it happened. Too young to remember. His parents were the ones who called the police." She rubbed Nivea Creme on her hands, massaging it into her fingers and slender wrists. "His earlobes are attached," she said, "and you know you can't trust people with attached earlobes."

I reached up and flopped my earlobes back and forth. My thumbs fit into the V-shaped gaps between the bottom of my earlobes and the sides of my head. Renate was touching her earlobes too. When Frau Brocker had first shared her theory about ears and trustworthiness with me, I'd counted the kids in my class with attached earlobes. Nearly half of them, including the principal, had earlobes that were connected in a smooth line to the sides of their heads.

"Tell us about Hans-Jürgen's trial," Renate asked, though we'd heard all about it just a few days ago.

"It lasted nine days." Frau Brocker had arrived early at the courthouse every morning to join the line of people waiting to get in. "The day he was committed to the asylum in Grafenberg," she said, "I was sitting in the first row."

Grafenberg was a half hour's drive from where we lived. It was known for two things: a spectacular forest and the insane asylum where Trudi Montag's mother had died. The sprawling buildings lay encircled by a high wall with curved glass splinters embedded in the mortar; yet, Hans-Jürgen had escaped from there last February, quite likely shredding his clothes and hands as he climbed the wall and hoisted himself over the top. For a few days his photo had appeared in the paper, but soon it had been replaced by politics and sports, and I'd forgotten all about him.

Until now. Headlines claimed the police were following new leads. The grainy pictures showed a man with a dark beard and blazing eyes who, Renate and I agreed, looked like Simon Peter, the most handsome apostle in *The Last Supper* mural above the altar of St. Martin's Church.

We wondered where we would hide out if the police were looking for us. The basement of the elementary school was a good possibility—no one was allowed down there except the janitor who took care of the furnace. Perhaps Hans-Jürgen was even hiding in the barn at his parents' farm. We thought of sneaking into the Braunmeiers' barn to see if we could find him, but we figured the police had already searched the obvious places. Besides—his parents were the ones who'd turned him in before.

It occurred to me that the best disguise would be a nun's habit: if Hans-Jürgen shaved off his beard, only a portion of his face would be exposed.

"He might be right in the Theresienheim," I told Renate.

But she shook her head until her hair flew around her shoulders. "The other nuns would know," she said with absolute certainty. "They would."

Convinced Hans-Jürgen was somewhere close by, we sat on our windowsills at night, writing lists of suspicious persons—anyone who passed our houses after eight. Sometimes, from two blocks away, came the howling of Emma Müller's chained poodle. Across the street from my bedroom window, the branches of the Talmeisters' cherry tree bent under the weight of the fruit. They were too high to reach from the sidewalk, and when the wind tore them from the tree, they exploded where they hit the sidewalk. Sparrows and pigeons picked at the dark red pulp, but most of it blotched the sidewalk like the evidence of a massacre, smeared lumps of red around bleached kernels that looked like bone fragments.

We kept adding to our list of hideouts, and the one that finally made the most sense was the abandoned flour mill with its crumbling brick arches and rotting floorboards. It had been destroyed during the war, and no one had bothered to restore it. Surrounded by woods and swamps, the huge cluster of rooms—some of them open to the sky—centered around a wide chimney.

To get to the old mill we had to ride our bicycles north, past the dump that was three kilometers from the middle of Burgdorf. In the moist air our skin felt clammy. Just before we reached the dump, the blacktop ended and our tires bounced along the narrow road with its slabs of broken pavement and rutted tire tracks. Renate's legs were too thin to hold up her white knee socks, and they dribbled down in uneven rolls above her black patent leather shoes. Though she pumped the pedals as hard as she could, her polio leg never seemed to keep up with her strong leg.

We biked to the mill almost every day that summer, and each time we heard the birds before we saw them rise in a tattered veil above the mounds of garbage. To startle them, I'd ring my bicycle bell, which Karin Baum's grandfather had given me long before my parents had forbidden me to go to his bicycle shop.

Sometimes we saw the town truck dump its load, and we pinched our nostrils as the stench mingled with the refuse already settling into decay. Some of the birds flew close enough to touch, had we wanted to. Depending on the direction of the wind, the smell followed us as we passed the dump and pedaled our bikes to the mill.

Tied under my bike seat was the coil of clothesline I'd taken from our basement. We searched the dense woods around the ancient brick structure, trying to avoid the patches of nettles that stung our legs and the swampy areas that sucked our shoes down and filled them with mud.

Thistles with purple flowers grew along the walls. Though the cold vaults of the arched stone building we shouted, "Hans-Jürgen . . . Hans-Jürgen . . . " clutching long sticks which we would hide inside the chimney before leaving. Cellar stairs dropped off into gaping holes of darkness, a thick darkness that wrapped itself around the amber beams of our flashlight when we pointed them to the ground. Sometimes we thought we heard footsteps moving away from us. Our plan was to strike Hans-Jürgen's head with our sticks before he had a chance to shoot us. He'd sink to the ground, a puzzled expression on his face as his eyes glazed over. For at least ten minutes he'd be unconscious—plenty of time to tie him up with the clothesline.

By the time school started in September, we had decided to become detectives when we grew up; we knew we had a special ability to imagine ourselves into the criminal mind. We kept our search for Hans-Jürgen secret from the other kids, especially from Rolf Brocker, who came to our apartment some days after school and then left with his mother around five. He'd only laugh at us, and then he'd tell Manfred Weiler. The two of them would steal our ideas, catch the murderer, and get all the publicity.

On weekends we rode our bikes to the old mill, and during the week we planned our detective work. In Renate's room we developed a secret language we'd sing out aloud in case Hans-Jürgen caught one of us. Vowels stayed the same, but consonants were doubled with an *o* in the middle. *Murderer* became *mom u ror dod e ror e ror*. The captured one—I always pictured Renate in this position, her back against Hans-Jürgen, his forearm across her throat —would chant the code loud enough for me to hear and rush for help.

We'd close her door so her brother, Adi, couldn't hear us practice our language. Wind stirred her lace curtains with the pattern of dolls holding hands. Above her bed hung a framed poster of Burgdorf taken from an airplane: the major streets seemed to form the pattern of a many-pointed star, its center at St. Martin's Church, as if someone had designed all the paths to lead there.

Some afternoons Renate and I plotted our strategy in the basement while sitting on crates next to the apple shelves. When it was warm outside, we played with marbles in the backyard, our right index fingers black where we'd lined them up against the ground to push marbles into the hole.

The backyard was bordered by our L-shaped building and a fence. Together they formed a square that could only be entered through one of the house's two entrances. The first floor, except for the section where we lived, contained stores: Neumaier's pharmacy, the optician, the hardware store, and Anton Immers's butcher shop. Above them were eighteen apartments. In one of them lived Manfred Weiler with his mother and two big sisters. Sometimes he watched us from his kitchen window. That fall, his old dachshund, Ola, had a false pregnancy and chose our marble hole to lie in. Her belly hot and taut, she growled and snapped at us each time we tried to move her.

"Hans-Jürgen . . . Hans-Jürgen . . . "

Our voices echoed through the empty rooms. Piles of brick and dirt lay in the corners. Renate walked close to me, clutching our coil of rope. It was a cloudy Saturday afternoon, and the air felt cool and damp. Our bare arms brushed, and we jumped apart, alarmed. Green shards from bottles glinted where our flashlights struck them. Weeds and moss trailed from gaps in the walls.

"Hans-Jürgen . . . Hans-Jürgen . . . "

In some of the rooms trees had forced their way through

the floor. They were stunted, except for one oak whose limbs pushed themelves beyond the old roof line of the mill. Sometimes a ray of wind trapped itself in the tangle of branches and thrust its way out, startling us and showering us with leaves.

The last Tuesday of November Hans-Jürgen Braunmeier was caught inside a movie theater in Düsseldorf, watching a Romy Schneider film. In the newspaper Renate and I read that, until four days before his arrest, he'd been hiding out at the mill. Though I wanted to tell my parents how close we'd come to finding the murderer, I knew it would be a mistake. They'd confine me to my room or forbid me to leave the street. They wouldn't understand that Renate and I had the special ability to imagine ourselves into the criminal mind.

Whenever I remember Renate and me searching through the empty building, I hear the sound of our voices as we call Hans-Jürgen's name. *He stands close by, half hidden by a crumbling archway. In the oak tree across the wall, wind rushes under the branches like a quick beam of light, and a swarm of leaves blows across the wall in a straight path. Hans-Jürgen lifts his face and one of the brittle shapes pushes against his cheek, twirls, then sinks down by his feet. He blinks. His hands are empty and scarred from his escape across the Grafenberg wall. He leans forward, head tilted as if listening. Any moment he might step toward us in response to our call.*

✐ Veronika

Frail, my mother said when she talked about her college friend Veronika. *Frail*—a word that meant black hair cropped short, long hands with many rings, soft flowing dresses. Whenever Veronika stayed at the sanatorium in Oberkassel, my mother and I would visit her on Sunday afternoons. A guard would open the gate, and we'd drive down a lane bordered by lilacs until we reached the building. If the weather was warm, we sat with Veronika in wicker chairs on the lawn and one of the attendants, young men in white trousers and shirts, served us lemonade in thick glasses. The front of the sanatorium was an old villa with turrets and a stained-glass window above the carved door, but its back was a concrete addition with recessed windows too small for anyone to squeeze through.

My mother and Veronika had met when both of them were students at the Art Academy in Düsseldorf. While my mother painted landscapes, Veronika drew charcoal sketches of people caught in one urgent, yet graceful motion that seemed to carry them forward as in a film. Her sketches reminded me of pictures I'd seen in one of my Oma's book of Pompeii, victims captured in their last

movement before they were killed by the eruption of Ve-
suvius. Hardened molds of ashes and rain had preserved
the shapes of the bodies long after the flesh had disinte-
grated.

In my mother's studio hung a photo of her and Veronika,
taken when they were nineteen, my mother tall and blond
and smiling, while Veronika, nearly a head shorter, gazed
seriously into the lens, her skin translucent, her neck long
and slim. Sometimes I stared into the mirror and wished I
looked frail like Veronika. At thirteen, I was the second-
tallest girl in my class. The boys in schools liked the girls
who were pretty and frail. When Veronika was a girl, she
must have had dozens of boyfriends. She'd married twice,
the first time a sculptor whom she'd divorced, then an Italian musician from whom she'd separated a few years before. She'd left Rome and moved to Düsseldorf, where she
rented an apartment with a loft that overlooked the Rhein,
but the Italian still sent her expensive handbags and matching shoes for her birthdays.

Veronika was the only divorced person I knew. She and
Matthias Berger were the only adults who let me call them
by their first names. With others it was always Herr or
Frau or Fräulein. I liked being with Veronika, even during
those visits at the sanatorium when she couldn't remember
my name. Turning the rings on her elegant fingers, she'd
sit there smiling at me, asking me who I was.

On days when she couldn't speak at all, her head would
jerk forward as though she were trying to make the words
fall from her mouth, and I'd think of the thousands of
unspoken words crowding inside her, wishing I could help
her release them. I'd feel my neck and shoulders tighten,
my lips moving as if, somehow, I could form those words
for her.

The doctors knew how to set free all those words, and
whenever Veronika was well enough to leave the hospital,
she'd move back into her apartment. She was beginning to

support herself with her drawings: two galleries in Düsseldorf exhibited them, and the *Rheinische Post* printed a full-page interview and photos of her work.

Once or twice a month she took a cab to Burgdorf and came to our house for dinner. Those evenings I wasn't allowed to have seconds because my parents, as soon as we'd helped ourselves, would carry the food back to the kitchen, wrap it, and store it in the refrigerator.

I discovered the reason for my parents' odd behavior one Sunday afternoon. Red and yellow leaves lay on the walk to our front door, glistening in the rain. From my bedroom window I watched a cab let Veronika off at the curb. She almost slipped on the leaves when she saw me waving to her. Quickly, I ran to the front door and opened it.

"Hanna." She smiled at me and untied the belt of her white hooded trenchcoat. On her thin face were raindrops, and she wiped them off with one hand.

"I was waiting for you."

She reached into her soft leather bag and handed me a flat package. "For you." Her fingers were smudged with charcoal.

I took off the wrapping paper. Inside was a blue diary with a lock on the front. And a key. "It's beautiful." I unlocked it and turned the unlined pages.

My mother came from the living room and held Veronika's face between her hands. "You look good," she said. "Real good."

Veronika laughed, a happy, embarrassed laugh. "So do you," she said and gave my mother a hug.

I knew what my mother meant: when Veronika was well, her face was wide open and smooth, but when she was in the sanatorium, it drew itself into tight fragments and lines that made her entire head appear smaller.

I went ahead of them into the dining room. Earlier, I'd helped my mother set the table with the hand-painted china that had belonged to her grandmother. In the middle of the white tablecloth sat a silver tray with six pieces of pastry, each of them different, filled with whipped cream and fruit. My mother had let me pick them out at the bakery.

Before pouring coffee for Veronika and herself, my mother added some coffee to my milk, turning it a soft caramel color.

"Where's Klaus?" Veronika asked.

"A chess tournament," my mother said. "In Köln. He went with Günther Stosick and two others from the chess club." She held out the pastry tray to Veronika. "You get first choice today."

Veronika lifted a piece to her plate. I ate slowly, savoring the whipped cream against the roof of my mouth as I tried to think how to start my diary; the first entry had to be significant; it couldn't be just anything. Their heads close together, Veronika and my mother talked and laughed, one voice soft, the other clear and just a bit louder.

When the phone rang in the kitchen, my mother got up to answer it. I separated my last layer of pastry with my fork. Suddenly I heard a choking sound. Veronika—her lower lip sucked in, her cheeks hollow, she took ragged breaths as she stared at the pastry tray.

"Veronika?"

She blinked, her eyes large, frightened.

"Would you like another piece?" I didn't know what else to say.

She didn't answer.

What if she had forgotten again how to speak? "Here," I said, "let me get one for you."

As I reached for a piece with chocolate shavings, Veronika's left hand shot out and her thin fingers dug themselves into my wrist. With her other hand she grasped the pastry I was about to give her, opened her mouth wide, and rammed all of it in at once. Whipped cream covered her chin; cherry filling ran down her neck and onto her lace collar. I couldn't look away as she shoved the other two pastries and the half-eaten piece from my mother's plate into her mouth, swallowing so hard that the skin on her neck stretched.

When she was finished, her mouth pushed into a smile. I tried to pull free of her, but she wouldn't let go of my wrist. As we stared at each other, her pupils seemed to expand until the fear was gone and, strangely, in those dark centers I saw myself—taller and older—as if protected forever in her sketches. She had never drawn me; yet, a whole sequence of images emerged as clearly as if she were flipping the pages of her sketchbook. Knowing how she saw me, how she would draw me, took away my uneasiness and made me feel safe and close to her.

We sat like this for a while. When my mother walked back into the dining room, her blue eyes turned dark, but not angry.

"Veronika?" Gently, she pried the fingers from my wrist. "Are you all right, Hanna?"

I nodded and hugged my burning wrist.

She laid her hands on Veronika's shoulders. Brought her face close. "Hanna is all right."

Veronika kept smiling.

"Hanna is all right. Do you hear me?"

"Yes." Veronika nodded.

My mother reached across the table, touched my cheek lightly. "Please, would you wait in your room?"

"But why—"

"I'll be there," she whispered. "As soon as I can. I promise."

I didn't turn on the light in my room. Standing by the window, I leaned my forehead against the cool glass, trying to evoke the images I'd seen in Veronika's eyes, but they wouldn't come back to me. Most of the trees along our street were already bare, their dark branches reaching toward the sky which gradually turned a deeper shade of gray. I kept seeing Veronika's face as she'd shoved those pastries into her mouth. Why had she looked so frightened? And why had she caught my wrist? Something important had happened between us, but I didn't know what it was.

After nearly an hour, a cab pulled up outside. Our front door opened, then closed. My mother helped Veronika into the backseat, then spoke to the driver and handed him something. She stood in the rain until the cab drove off.

When she came into my room, she put one arm around me and drew me close. "Do you want to tell me what happened?"

I nodded, and after I'd told her, she looked at my wrist, which really didn't hurt anymore.

"Veronika loves you," she said. "Very much. She'd never want to do anything that could harm you. You see— she believed she was saving your life. Ever since she was a child, she has seen things that don't happen. Sometimes, when food is left on the table, she thinks she sees poison fall on it."

"Poison?"

"She believes she's the only one who can't die from the poison. That's why she ate all the pastries and wouldn't let you have any."

I wondered what the poison looked like to Veronika, if it was a fine powder or a liquid.

"Sometimes she flushes food down the toilet so nobody else can eat it. If the phone—"

"Is that why you always get everything off the table so quickly?"

My mother nodded. "I wish this hadn't happened, Hanna."

As she held me, I felt as if nothing bad could ever happen to either of us, and for the first time I understood the meaning of *frail*.

From then on, whenever Veronika came to our house, I became my mother's accomplice in whisking everything off the table as soon as we'd helped ourselves. I wished I could ask her about the poison, where she thought it came from, and why it couldn't harm her, and as I held back questions I sensed I shouldn't ask I imagined those plaster casts of people killed in Pompeii—but instead of ashes and rain, a fine shower of poison fell on them, corrupting their flesh but sustaining their form in one final absolution.

One evening, while my father showed Veronika some photos he'd taken of us on the island Wangerooge the previous summer, a chocolate cake disappeared from the table. Veronika's Italian handbag bulged and wouldn't close. After a few minutes she excused herself and went to the bathroom. We heard the toilet flush. Twice.

My parents glanced at each other. "It's easier for her if she thinks we don't know," my father said to me.

Veronika went back to the hospital three days before Christmas. When my mother and I drove out to visit her, the front lawn was covered with snow. One of the attendants called her to the visitors' room where a Christmas tree with candles and handmade ornaments had been set up. When Veronika unwrapped the presents we'd brought for her—a yellow angora sweater and a Mozart tape—her fingers moved slowly as if she had to figure out how to untie the ribbons. My mother reached across me and helped her take off the wrapping.

One of the attendants served us *Lebkuchen* and spicy tea. Around the Christmas tree sat other people in small groups, talking in hushed voices, and I could tell who the patients were because they were the ones opening presents.

Veronika did not speak and sat stiffly without leaning against the backrest of the sofa. Her face was small, the skin under her eyes pink and creased. Her long neck didn't look strong enough to bear the weight of her head. When I touched her hand, her eyes filled with tears, but then she smiled and I knew that soon she'd be well again as she had all those other times.

In the years to come, Veronika would become famous,

not just in our area of the Rheinland, but throughout Germany and most of Europe. Yet, once she was known, the media acted as though her success had happened overnight, and several collectors prided themselves on having discovered her. All of this mattered very little to Veronika; what counted for her was the reaction of those who were drawn to her sketches as if responding to some fleeting image they recognized within themselves.

Baby Mansion

When Karin Baum, who was in seventh grade with me, got so big that people could tell she was carrying a baby, it didn't take her parents long to discover that her grandfather had made her pregnant. They closed the old man's bicycle shop and sent him to live with his unmarried brother in München, while Karin was taken to the baby mansion, a white villa with a clay-tiled roof four kilometers from Burgdorf. It was a safe place where a family could store a daughter who was gaining weight around the middle, store her for a few months, and then take her back home, slender again as though nothing had changed.

During those months of preparing for birth, the pregnant girls took care of the babies who already lived at the mansion and waited for adoption or for their mothers to finally take them home. Most of these children were in limbo: their mothers had not decided for or against adoption—they'd simply left them there. And so they stayed, growing beyond the age where people wanted to adopt them, moving from the nursery to the room of the one-year-olds to the two-plus dormitory.

On Sunday afternoons some of the unwed mothers visited their children. They gave them bright toys, carried them through the rose garden behind the mansion, played with them on the lawn that surrounded the marble fountain. A few of them brought their boyfriends. Occasionally a girl's parents came along. In the lobby of the baby mansion a table covered with a linen cloth was set up with refreshments. A pregnant girl poured coffee and offered the visitors leaf-shaped cookies from a silver platter.

It rained the first Sunday in June when my mother and I drove out to see Karin. It was my idea to visit her, but once we were there, I didn't know what to say or where to look. In the three weeks since she'd left school she had grown even bigger; the pleats of her loose dress spread above her stomach as she led us into the visitors' room. Her straight brown hair, which used to hang down her back, had been cut; it exposed her earlobes, and the center part made her look serious, older.

After sitting with us for a few minutes, my mother stood up. "I'll be back in a while," she said and left the room before I could stop her.

Karin pulled off a shred of skin next to her left thumbnail. "So—" she said, examining her thumb, "how's school?"

"All right." My neck felt stiff from the effort of not staring at her belly. "How's—you know . . . living here?"

She shrugged and hid with me in the embarrassed silence that folded around us until I felt as though my body, too, were swollen. Voices drifted in from the lobby. A young girl's laugh. The sound of a door. A few times Karin reached up as if to twist a strand of hair but touched her shoulder instead.

When my mother finally returned, Karin seemed as relieved as I felt. "Let us know if you need anything," my mother offered.

"Thank you, Frau Malter," Karin said.

Before starting our car in the parking lot, my mother sat with her eyes closed. The collar of her cotton shirt was turned up, catching strands of blond hair between the blue material and her skin.

"What's wrong?" I asked.

"I should have known. . . . " She opened her eyes. Lit a cigarette. One hand on the steering wheel, she maneuvered the car out of the lot. She drove fast. Too fast. "I should have talked to her parents that day," she said, "not just to the old man."

All at once I remembered the white coating on the back of my doll's eyes, the makeshift surgery on the dining room table, and I was seized by the loss of a friendship that had ended the year Karin and I were seven.

Until then, the bicycle shop had been a magic place for me, filled with the fairy tales Karin's grandfather had told me, warm and bright even in winter, strangely familiar with its faint smell of machine oil and black rubber that drifted up the stairs and wove itself into the apartment above, through the kitchen, and even into Karin's room.

Karin was my best friend before Renate came to our school. We sat next to each other in Frau Behrmeier's second-grade class. Her grandfather knew all the fairy tales from the Brothers Grimm book: *Rapunzel, Hänsel und Gretel, Rumpelstilzchen* . . . He told those stories in a voice that could drop from the roar of a dragon to the whisper of a princess.

An old man with wide shoulders, he had a squat build that seemed to grow closer to the floor each year. He lived above the shop with Karin and her parents. In the back pocket of his overalls he carried a rag for polishing the bikes on display. Oil stains spread across the backs of his hands like birthmarks, but the bicycles were spotless and gleamed under the many light bulbs he'd rigged from the ceiling.

He liked to stroke my hair and lift me on top of the glass counter between the cash register and the display of bicycle chains. The dark smell of oil and rubber clung to his olive skin and gray mustache.

Once he took Karin and me on a ferry trip to Kaiserswerth and from there on an excursion boat to the Altstadt, the old section of Düsseldorf. At an outdoor cafe with round tables, he ordered *Früchtebecher* for us—layers of banana ice cream with pineapple chunks and whipped cream —and Berliner Weisse—beer with raspberry syrup foaming in a goblet—for himself. Whenever flies tried to land on the checkered tablecloth, he swatted them away with his broad hands. A maple tree on the sidewalk was shedding some of its double-winged seeds, and we caught them as they twirled down like propellers and stuck them to our upper lips like his mustache.

One Monday afternoon, when I came looking for Karin at the shop, her grandfather told me her mother had taken her to Mahler's department store in Düsseldorf.

"Shopping," he said.

"Can I stay?"

He pulled a rag from his pocket and wiped his hands. "Here," he said and lifted me onto the counter next to a flowerpot shaped like a duck. It was filled with real ferns and red plastic daisies.

"Will you tell me a story?"

"How old are you now, Hanna?"

I smiled at him. "You know."

"Come on. Tell me. How old are you?"

"Seven. Remember? You gave me a bicycle bell on my last birthday."

"Seven." He nodded as if not one bit surprised. In the ridges of his cheeks and across his neck lay a film of dust.

"A big girl like you . . . doesn't wet her pants anymore, does she?"

My neck felt hot. "Only babies wet their pants."

He brought his face close to mine and peered into my eyes. "You're sure?" His breath was moist against my face. Hair sprouted from his ears and nose.

"I don't. I never do."

On the wall behind him hung shiny bike parts and black tires. Two air pumps were propped against the lower part of the wall.

"Really sure?" His hand reached under my skirt and pressed against the dry patch of cotton panties between my legs. "You're sure now you don't wet your pants?"

"I told you." Squirming away from him, I slid from the counter and ran toward the door.

"Wait." His voice sounded as if he were afraid. "The story. I'll tell you a—"

But I kept running. Down the sidewalk that shimmered white in the afternoon sun. Across the empty street. Around the corner. Past the elementary school where the Hansen bakery truck was parked. Kept running until I reached our building. In the kitchen Frau Brocker was ironing my plaid dress. Rolf sat at the table, drawing a black truck.

"Where's Karin?" Fine beads of sweat coated Frau Brocker's forehead as she moved the iron across the material. Her brown hair lay in new curls around her head, and she wore bright red lipstick.

"I don't know." I darted past her into my room and closed the door.

"Hanna?" she called after me, but I pretended not to hear.

I sat on my bed and looked out the window into the backyard with the chicken coop and the high iron rods over which the women from the apartments laid their carpets every Friday and beat them with long rattan paddles. The fence that closed off the backyard had several rows of chain links that didn't match the lower section. Until two years ago, when I was first allowed out on my own, my father had drawn the fence higher each year; still, I'd managed to climb across it on my many trips to explore the neighborhood. It had started when, at age three, I'd been found sitting on Emma Müller's bed two blocks away, playing with her dolls.

I didn't play with dolls anymore. They were boring. I liked books; yet, people kept giving me dolls. Frau Brocker had lined them up on the shelf next to my bed, from the tallest one, Inge, to a finger-sized doll named Birgit.

Inge was made of celluloid and had blue glass eyes that closed when I tilted her back. Her eyelashes lay against her cheeks until I moved her whole body forward again and then her eyes clicked open, hard and glossy. When I pulled the eyelashes, the blue disappeared once more, and I wondered what the doll saw inside her head.

I carried her to the open window where the light was brighter. Such a stupid-looking doll—all stiff and pink. As I pushed my fingers against the eyes to test how far in they could go, they moved back from their sockets, then snapped right back. I pushed again to see how they were held in place. Then again, a little harder . . . Suddenly the eyes disappeared into the head. Just like that. I shook the doll, her face pointing toward the floor, but the eyes wouldn't drop back into their sockets; they only rattled inside the celluloid head.

"Frau Brocker," I shouted, then covered my mouth. I didn't want her to see the doll, didn't want anyone to see.

The door opened. I wanted to hide the doll, but I couldn't move.

"What's the matter?" My father came into my room.

The doll hung from my hand. I thought he'd get angry

at me for breaking her eyes, but instead he lifted her from my hands as if she were a newborn kitten.

"How did it happen?"

I started to cry.

He brought one arm around my shoulders. "I'm sure it was an accident."

"I don't even like dolls." I wiped the back of my hand across my eyes and nose. My stomach ached from letting him believe it was an accident.

"I think we can fix her. At least we can try. All right?"

My father had finished with his patients for the day and took most of that afternoon to restore the blue eyes to their proper location. With thin pliers, black thread, and tweezers he sat at our dining room table, fishing through the empty sockets for the eyeballs. I sat across from him and handed him instruments as he called out their names. The light above the table made his scalp look shiny where his reddish hair had thinned; yet, his beard was full and curly as if all the growing had happened in those hairs.

Around five o'clock large raindrops began falling rapidly, splattering the windows. On the wall between the two windows hung my mother's painting of the Sternburg, the one she'd been working on the day she fell in love with my father. She'd painted the Sternburg many times since then, but in this picture the drawbridge was down, spanning the moat that circled the old farm. The light in the painting would change: on sunny days it looked almost transparent while in the evenings, when we turned on the lamps, it took on an amber sheen as if warmed by the light surrounding it.

My father still had on the white jacket that he wore when he drilled people's teeth. When Frau Brocker and Rolf came into the dining room to tell us they were leaving for the day, he interrupted his operation to praise Rolf's picture of the black truck. Frau Brocker stopped by the window, frowning at the rain. Her hair was covered with a plastic scarf to protect her permanent.

I ran my fingers along the edge of the tablecloth and found the knife she'd hidden under the beige linen to ward off the lightning. After they left, my father bent back over the doll. From time to time he blinked. His breathing was slow, measured. When he finally pulled the blue eyes from one of the sockets, they were connected by two wire loops that formed the number eight, and I was disappointed to see that their backs were coated with a white substance that felt like hardened flour against my fingertips. My father glued the eyes into the sockets, holding them in slings of thread until the glue set; then he cautiously pulled out the threads and applied more glue around the seams where the glass joined the pink celluloid. Though he dabbed the corners with an old handkerchief, some of the glue hardened into tiny drops that looked like tears.

"Here." He handed me the doll. "I think that's the best we can do."

The blue eyes stared at me and stayed open although the doll was lying on its back.

"She's almost like new," I tried to convince myself as I held the stiff doll in my arms. But she was not like new: she couldn't close her eyes anymore, and inside her head the backs of her eyes were blind.

Around eight my father left to play chess at the Burgdorf chess club, which met at Herr Stosick's house. When my mother tucked me in and sat on the edge of my bed, my stomach felt even worse from not telling her and my father how I'd broken the doll.

"Karin's grandfather forgot how old I was," I blurted out instead. "He thought I still wet my pants."

She shook her head. "Why would he . . . ?"

I tried to laugh away my uneasiness. "But then he checked, and now he knows I don't."

My mother sat very still. The skin around her nose became white as though all the color had drained to her neck. She laid one hand against my cheek and asked softly, "Are you all right?" And when I nodded, she gathered me into her arms and said, "Will you please tell me? Everything?"

I told her about pushing out the doll's eyes and that I was sorry, but she wanted to know more about Karin's grandfather touching my underpants. As I told her, she held me gently and said that what he'd done to me was wrong. "Very wrong." Then she got up and put on her raincoat and walked to the bicycle shop.

I kept the light on and lay with my arms folded under my head, counting my breaths in the empty apartment. On the shelf next to my bed sat Inge, her blue eyes wide open, opaque drops of hardened glue in the corners of the sockets.

My mother didn't tell me what she'd said to Karin's grandfather when she came back into my room, but she asked me, "Will you promise to stay away from the bicycle shop?"

I thought of the bicycle parts reflecting the lights, thought of the cool glass counter and felt the sudden loss of a place I didn't want to return to.

"It's a filthy place," my mother said.

Yet it was also warm and bright and magic.

"Promise to stay away from there?"

I nodded, suddenly relieved.

"Karin can play with you here. Anytime." My mother bent to kiss my forehead. "I'm glad you told me what happened."

My friendship with Karin Baum straggled on through that fall and winter. We played in the schoolyard or at our house, but not in the bicycle shop. And the following spring Renate became my new best friend.

Some things are too complex to name, to separate into safe units labeled good or bad, and it becomes simpler to discard them entirely. I think that's what happened to my friendship with Karin, and it wasn't until she carried her grandfather's baby, that I came to understand the impact of losing her.

My first visit to the baby mansion was so awkward that I felt reluctant to return when my mother wrapped a box of pralines and a book for Karin a week later. But something happened that second Sunday afternoon in the visitors' room, something I couldn't even remember afterward except that Karin had laughed at something I'd said. Somehow that moment wiped out the embarrassment between us, and when my mother suggested the two of us take a walk through the rose garden, Karin and I left her in the visitors' room and walked along the manicured paths.

The people in Burgdorf didn't approve of my mother taking me to the baby mansion; they approved even less of me riding my bicycle there some days after school, as if unwed pregnancies were contagious. But the only thing that was contagious was our need to fill each other in on what had happened to us during those years we hadn't been friends. Sure, we'd sat in the same classroom, and a few times we'd played pranks, unhinging garden doors all over Burgdorf, but that was not the same.

And so we talked for hours—in the visiting room, the rose garden, and the nursery where Karin worked. We talked about friends and school and boys and parents. But not about her baby. And certainly not about her grandfather, although I thought about the old man whenever I tried not to look at Karin's belly.

She was assigned to work each afternoon in the dormitory of the one-year-olds, a long, airy room with rows of cribs. When school closed for summer vacation, I asked Karin if I could help her with the babies, and she got permission from Frau Doktor Korten, who ran the baby mansion, for me to help two afternoons a week. The doctor had small hands and a gentle voice, but she was so heavy and tall that she could fill a door frame with her bulk. Her gray hair was parted down the middle like Karin's, but pulled back into a low braided knot. When she walked into the nursery—a white smock over her flowered silk dress—most of the children raised their arms toward her.

Two sixteen-year old girls, Anita and Grete, worked with us. We fed the babies, took off their diapers and shirts, gave them baths in high sinks shaped like miniature tubs. We laughed when they splashed us and when we sprinkled powder on their bottoms and bellies.

Anita was at the baby mansion for the second time. She'd given up her first child for adoption. One afternoon, when Anita told us she was going to keep this baby, Karin surprised me by saying she was keeping hers too. Until then she hadn't said a word about it.

"Hanna is going to help me care for the baby after school." She reached for my hand and held it against her belly.

I felt the baby move under my palm like a sleeper stretching after a long rest.

For the first time we talked about names for her child. She liked Adelheid for a girl and Siegfried for a boy, though I tried to tell her that Martina and Joachim were better names. If my brother, Joachim, had lived, he'd be eleven years old.

A few of the babies had something wrong with them: Andrea was blind, and Franz only had a thumb and little finger on his left hand. Renate told me that marrying a cousin could get you a baby with two heads or a clubfoot. Her mother, the midwife, had helped bring all kinds of deformed babies into the world. "A grandfather," Renate told me, "is even a closer relative than a cousin." She probably said this because she was upset at me for spending so much time with Karin; yet, I couldn't help imagining the baby behind the wall of Karin's belly, waiting backstage like an actor with a frightful mask.

But when the child was born in September, she wasn't ugly or deformed. She had fine black hair and blue-gray eyes and thin fingers that gripped my thumb the afternoon I was allowed to hold her. She was two days old, and I felt a jolt of love that stunned me into silence as I stood with her in the newborn nursery. I carried her to the French doors and lifted her close to the glass so she could see the rose garden and the fountain. I pictured myself taking her for walks in a wicker carriage. Now that Karin's grandfather didn't live above the bicycle shop anymore, I'd be allowed back into the apartment. Karin and I would play with her, give her baths, sing to her.

But Karin's parents wouldn't let her bring the baby home. They talked about adoption. At first Karin cried and refused to leave the mansion, but one evening, after a long talk with Frau Doktor Korten, she let her father pick her up. When I visited Karin, I felt strange walking through the bicycle shop. It had been leased to a young man without a mustache, but the same old smell of tires and machine oil hung about the apartment and opened an odd sensation in my stomach.

Karin sat on her bed, a stack of closed books and magazines on her blanket. Her hair was stringy. "They wouldn't even let me name her." She started to cry.

"They can't do that." I sat on the edge of her bed. "If you don't sign the adoption papers, they can't give her to anyone."

"But then she'll have to stay there."

"We'll visit her. And after a while—maybe your parents will change their minds."

"They won't." She shook her head. "I know they won't."

Right then I decided to name the baby Martina even if she got adopted and her new parents chose a different name for her, and the next afternoon I rode my bike to the baby mansion and offered to help in the newborn nursery on weekends.

"Let's go for a walk in the garden," Frau Doktor Korten suggested. As she moved along the paths, soft ripples went through her body and made the flowers in her dress shiver. She told me I'd helped Karin a lot while she'd been there, but that it would be better for me if I didn't come back. "And for the baby," she said. "You've become too attached." Beneath her skirt her thighs made a soft, slapping sound.

"Martina can sleep in my room," I said to my parents at dinner. "Frau Brocker is here all day anyhow, and I'll take care of the baby after school."

"I know you love her a lot," my mother said, "but it wouldn't be good for her if she stayed in Burgdorf—for her or for Karin. She'd only be reminded of her all the time."

My father laid one hand on my arm. "Try to understand. You're too young to take on that kind of responsibility."

"But Karin could visit her here. She'd help—I know she would."

My mother shook her head.

"If you adopted her . . . I mean, if Joachim hadn't died—"

"But he did, Hanna," my father said softly.

They both assured me that Martina would find a family of her own who really wanted her, that it would be better for her to live away from here, but I didn't want to listen: all I knew was how unfair it was that Martina should be punished for who her father was. Though my parents didn't say so, I knew it was all about that. Martina had been banned from Karin's life, just as I had been banned from the bicycle shop. And all because of Karin's grandfather—not because either of us had done anything wrong.

When Karin came back to school, the other kids didn't quite know what to say to her, especially Renate. I tried to do things with them together, but since they didn't like each other, I split my time between them, riding bikes with Renate or sitting in Karin's room above the bicycle shop.

Karin seemed so much older than the other kids, and when I was with her, I felt almost grown up. She was thin again and the ends of her hair touched her shoulders. Her parents hadn't taken her back to the baby mansion—not even once —and she wasn't allowed to ride her bicycle there.

"They'd find out," she said when I tried to talk her into riding out there with me one Saturday morning. "And I promised not to."

Martina was two months old when Karin's parents convinced her to sign the adoption papers. When she told me the next day in school, it struck me that, lately, entire days had gone by without my thinking of Martina, and I felt as if I'd been the one to abandon her.

"Maybe it is better for her," Karin said, "getting two parents who love her." But those words didn't sound like her own, and the skin around her eyes looked puffy.

I left her standing in the tiled hallway and ran out to the bicycle rack. The November sun stood low in the sky as I rode my bike to the baby mansion. I had to do something, but I didn't know what. When I tried to picture myself riding back, Martina in one arm, I couldn't see beyond that. My parents certainly wouldn't let me bring her home, and I couldn't just hide her in our basement. Some of the puddles along the way had glazed over with skins of ice that tore under my bicycle tires.

In back of the mansion the rosebushes had been pruned and the fountain turned off. I leaned my bike against a hedge and walked up the steps to the flagstone terrace. The French doors of the newborn nursery were locked. Martina's crib stood close to the glass panes: she lay on her back, awake; her black hair had grown fuller and looked as if someone had recently brushed it. A clean sheet covered her legs. Though her features hadn't changed, she seemed larger, stronger than the infant I'd held in my arms. She raised her right arm as if tracing an invisible sketch in the air, and I pressed my palms against the cool window squares, wishing I could feel the same love for her that I'd felt in the beginning, but all I could have was an odd sense of peace.

The Woman Who Would Not Speak

Manfred Weiler's father hung himself when Manfred was six years old. A few hours after he held Manfred out of the window of their third-floor apartment, he tied a length of rope to the cast-iron lamp in the kitchen and—while the rest of Burgdorf celebrated the passing of the old year, 1952—slipped the rope around his neck and stepped off a chair, though he didn't mean to.

One winter morning, years after his death, when Manfred and I were sitting in the same algebra class, I looked at him from the side and it was as if I could see his father's vicelike palms around his temples, holding him suspended above the night. I imagined those hands closing around my head, imagined the endless drop from the third floor to the packed dirt of the backyard, felt a cold surprise that made my spine and feet heavy, stiff, and felt the sudden rush of icy night air moving upward through my body.

But Manfred's father did not drop him.

He held him out of the kitchen window long enough to force his wife, Helga, to tell him where she'd hidden the grocery money, and then he pulled Manfred back into the kitchen and—gently—laid him on the floor.

The Weilers rented a small apartment on the third floor in the other arm of our L-shaped building. In the backyard Manfred and I learned to ride our tricycles. We fought. Played with his dachshund puppy, Ola, which his father had won in a poker game. Escaped together across the fence my father had raised to keep us safe, and ran to the playground of the Catholic school, which we were too young to attend.

When Manfred's father was sober, he gave us candy sticks and told us all about luck. "You have to believe in it if you want it to work." He'd pull us along on our tricycles by tying a frayed length of manila rope to our handlebars. He'd step into the loop and—the rope tight against his belly—he'd run while we screeched with laughter. Sometimes, when he had money and the bell of the Hansen bakery truck rang from the street, he bought us *Schnecken*, and we'd uncoil the glazed pastry ribbons so we could loosen the raisins with our tongues and eat them first.

Manfred's father had a chicken coop in the backyard, and whenever he slaughtered a chicken, he gave the feet to Manfred and me. We'd chase his older sisters down the stairs and around the yard, pulling the tendons that hung out like pieces of string and made the claws open and close.

One warm day in spring we let out one of the new chicks. Its legs were gawky, its feathers the color of lemon. Careful so it wouldn't get away from us, we played with it on the ground. It kept drawing its head back like an old man hunching up his shoulders against the wind. Though the sun was out, the earth was still moist from the night's rain, and whenever the chick staggered and fell, particles of dirt clung to its feathers.

It was Manfred's idea to give it a bath in one of the

puddles, but I was the one who held it submerged in the shallow water. While it tried to squirm from my hands, Manfred rubbed at the dirty spots. A few times it shrieked, but as its feathers plastered themselves against its body, the chick turned silent, skinny.

"It's stopped moving." I lifted it from the puddle.

Manfred splashed some water on its head. "Come on—you. Wake up."

Gauzy skin over the hills of its eyes, the chick lay in my palms. My stomach cramped as I tried to push the chick into Manfred's hands.

"You killed it!" He took a step back. "You'll be in trouble."

"I did not!"

"My father—" He started to cry.

"We—we can bury it."

He sniffled, ran the end of his sleeve under his nose. "Where?"

The chick felt limp, wet. "Over there." With my chin I motioned toward the white lilac bush outside my parents' bedroom window. "No one will find it under there."

The ground was soft enough to dig a shallow grave with our hands among the lilac shoots. We lowered the chick into the hole, covered it with dirt, and tried to flatten the mound with our hands.

"You better stomp it down." Manfred's face was streaked with dirt and tears.

"Not me. You do it."

Perhaps I only imagined the fine crunch of bones below his feet as he stepped on the small grave, but I felt certain I heard something as his soles left deep prints in the earth.

Though his father found out about the dead chick from Manfred's sister Margit, who'd watched us from their kitchen window, he didn't punish Manfred. Instead he sat with both of us on the back steps and made us promise not to open the door to the chicken coop again. He didn't even yell at us. It was one of those times when his eyes were clear and the sleeves of his shirt buttoned. He told us his luck was starting to come back—that he could feel it. I remember loving him for a brief time that day while we sat on the stone steps, loving him for his free laugh and the promise of luck and the excitement in his voice and the way the sun slanted on his blond hair and caught itself in his eyes.

And yet—many nights his shouts and the sounds of things breaking drifted across the yard. When we heard the cries of Manfred and his sisters, my mother turned on the light above our back door. Arms crossed, she stood by the window. The skin around her nostrils turned white, and she looked as if she were about to storm out of the apartment, through the dark backyard, and up the stairs to the Weiler's apartment.

Sometimes Manfred's mother knocked at our door, pale and silent and ashamed, a raincoat covering her nightgown. One of the children carried the short-legged brown dog. My mother spread sheets on the sofa for Frau Weiler, and my father blew up air mattresses for Manfred and his two older sisters.

Frau Weiler usually disappeared for a while and returned to her apartment where her husband lay snoring across the bed. Careful not to wake him, she located his trousers on the floor and found his shabby wallet. If he ever missed any of the fives or tens, he didn't say. Perhaps his wife's thefts gave him a sense of absolution. Perhaps he was too drunk to remember how much money he'd brought home. Resentful that he was forcing her to do something she detested, she kept taking the money to buy food and replace the children's outgrown clothes and shoes.

The night Herr Weiler hung himself is framed by facts which Frau Weiler later told the police and the neighbors;

yet, within that frame so much is left blank that each time I imagine what happened, the picture changes as I fill in details and try to hush my questions with answers that make sense.

That night—after he held his son from the window and after he found the money in his wife's summer shoes—Herr Weiler was stunned as he stood there with the bills in his hands. All at once he felt a lightness rolling up in his stomach—laughter. He tried to choke it, to disguise it as a coughing fit. *No.* It rolled and bounded from within him.

His wife crouched on the floor, her arms around their son. Both stared at him, their faces pale. The window was still open, letting in ice ribbons of wind. His daughters pressed against the wall furthest from him, one of them clutching the dachshund in her arms.

"I'm sorry," he wheezed, holding his sides. They stung. *Stop.* It made everything worse, knowing that he shouldn't laugh, but those sounds that rose from inside him were more powerful than he. He tried to straighten his face into serious lines as he moved toward the door. "I'm sorry," he said again and stumbled from the apartment.

As he entered the Traube, he felt his shoulders loosen, felt his body melt into the dark warmth of the bar. Smoke circled in irregular swirls to the wooden ceiling. The memory of his son's face between his hands tugged at him, but he didn't let it. This was real—the smell of tobacco and beer, the familiar faces. Chairs were moved closer together as his friends made room for him. He felt contentment as if it had a texture of its own, something he could almost touch and hold in his hands.

"He didn't seem different," his friends would say in the days to come whenever they talked about his death. "Not different at all."

When he lifted the heavy mug to his lips, it seemed to float. A pleasant glow started behind his cheekbones. Everything was smooth. When the others got ready to leave, he tried to convince them to have just one more. Half rising from his chair, he laid his hand on someone's coat sleeve, but the men were already on their way to the door. Heavily, he sank back. He was the only man sitting alone.

He motioned to the waiter. "A round for everyone."

Faces turned and glasses were raised toward him. But it wasn't as it had been before, and it didn't last.

"He was still there when we left," his friends would remind each other. "Alone at the table."

He got up, staggered to the door. In the cold night air he was caught in a sudden remorse that brought out the sharp smell of sweat all over his body. He didn't mean to hurt his son. He didn't mean it. He'd change. He'd tell Helga in the morning. But when he opened the apartment door, she was sitting at the table, hands folded on the bare wood.

"Manfred—" He swallowed hard. "Is Manfred all right?"

Her eyes, unwavering and huge, looked through him.

"Please," he said, "Helga?"

When she didn't answer, he rushed toward his son's bedroom. The shaft of ivory light that fell through the door from the kitchen didn't reach the bed. He bent closer, stopped. The breathing—he couldn't hear any breathing. In an instant it brought back to him the many times he'd gotten up in the middle of the night to check on his children when they were infants. All three were healthy; yet, he'd always had the fear that suddenly they might stop breathing. Invariably there would be that endless moment of straining to hear their breath, so faint he'd have to lay two fingers against their fragile necks to reassure himself.

But that was a long time ago and Manfred's breathing was usually strong. Herr Weiler threw back the covers. The bed was empty. So were his daughters' beds in the next room.

"Where are they?"

It seemed to cost Helga great effort to part her lips. "Where you can't hurt them."

"I would never hurt them. I'm sorry. I promise it won't happen again. I—" He lowered his face into his hands. His shoulders trembled as he waited for her to say that she forgave him.

But she remained silent.

His hands sank to the table where they lay close to hers, a terrible distance, a distance he saw in her eyes and the line of her chin and the stillness of her body.

"Here—the money—I'll give it back." He emptied the leftover bills and coins from his pocket, pushed them toward her on the table.

She didn't look at the money.

"Please, forgive me." Suddenly he was afraid that she would disappear like his children.

"You almost killed Manfred."

"I'm sorry." The fear tasted like iron in his mouth. If only he could think of something that would make her forgive him. "Maybe I should kill myself," he heard his voice, quick and high before he had time to think. "If you can't forgive me, I don't want to live."

She didn't speak.

He looked at the plaster ceiling with its threadlike cracks, at the massive cast iron lamp. "I'll hang myself."

Her hands, still folded, tightened.

"Please, Helga—"

Her eyes were dark.

In the closet he found the coil of manila rope. Placing his chair under the lamp, he stepped onto it, steadying himself with one hand on the back rest. She'd forgive him. She had to. All he needed was another chance to show her he could change. He tied a loop and guided the rope through it. His hands felt frozen. Throwing the other end of the rope over the top of the lamp, he pulled it until the noose was next to his face. The weight of the loop kept forcing the sliding noose down, and he had to adjust it to the right height before securing the rope to the lamp. Any moment now

Helga would stop him. Surely now she would have to tell him that she believed him, that she forgave him.

"Is this what you want?" he asked and opened the noose far enough to thrust his head through. It slid easily down to his neck, and he was surprised at its lightness. "Helga? It's up to you, Helga."

As a child he had liked to stand on the wine-red chair in his parents' living room, scanning the street far below where people and bicycles and cars moved in barely changing patterns; he became so familiar with the way things appeared from above that—even when he was outside and on the same level he knew what they looked like from a distance as if he had absorbed a double yet lucid exposure of their image.

He saw himself like that now, standing on the chipped kitchen chair, the rope loosely around his neck, its other end fastened to the lamp, and he was aware of every detail in the room at once: the blue and white linoleum squares, the fine cracks in the ceiling, the dog's water dish in the space below the sink. His cheeks ached. This was as far as he could go. He tried to postpone the moment when he would have to take off the noose and admit to Helga that even this was just another lie. If she gets up, he wagered, everything will be all right. If—if someone knocks at the door . . .

"Do you want me to die?"

She brought her folded hands to her face and opened them, ran them across her eyes as if to clear away a vision.

"Please, Helga, say something." He longed to touch her face, trace the lines that ran from the sides of her nose to the corners of her mouth. Sometimes at night, when she was asleep, he'd roll over on his right side and fit himself along the curve of her body. His left hand on her stomach, he'd bury his face against the back of her neck and breathe in the fresh, bitter scent of camomile; she rinsed her hair with tea she brewed from the yellow and white blossoms that grew along the Rhein. He'd cup her breasts with his hands, coaxing her from sleep toward the moment when she woke softly, her body aroused before her mind had cleared. It was always a gamble—depending on how she woke up. If it was too abrupt, she'd twist from his embrace and turn from him. In the morning she wouldn't even remember that he'd tried. But if her body awoke before her mind, she'd drowsily receive him, her hands moving down his back as her body arched up against him. Yet, sometimes his luck felt too flimsy and he couldn't take that chance. He'd get up instead, careful not to wake her as he adjusted the blanket around her shoulders.

"Helga, please, say something." He ran two fingers between the rope and his neck. How dark her eyes were. Didn't she see him at all or was she looking right through him? I'm just unlucky, he thought. Nothing ever goes right for me. Even my children are afraid of me. And Helga. She doesn't think I mean this. I'll show her. By God, I'll show her. Then she'll have to believe me. Then she'll—

Before he could stop himself, he stepped from the edge of the chair with his right foot. *No,* something within him screamed. *No. I didn't mean it.* But as he tried to regain his balance with his other foot, the chair toppled over, the sound of its fall like something crashing far away. *Put it back, Helga, put it back,* he wanted to cry, but his words were gagged. Falling, falling, he felt the noose tighten around his neck. His feet kicked, stretched for the floor, just out of reach. As his hands flew up to ease the pressure around his throat, he felt as though two large thumbs were pressing against his temples.

Through a whirl of red and yellow circles he saw Helga at a great distance, growing smaller, as her hands gripped the edge of the table. Faster the colors twirled, faster, becoming one with searing pain and lightness.

. . .

This is the only memory that's entirely mine about that night, a memory I don't have to expand with imagined details to make it whole: Manfred and his sisters sleeping with their dog, Ola, in our living room; Frau Weiler coming to our door early the next morning, her face chalky, her voice without tone as she tells her children and us: "It's all over now."

I remember the funeral, remember Margit's marriage to a florist from Oberkassel, Manfred's departure for military training in Frankfurt. But all that happened later. Much later. And whenever I think of Manfred's parents in their kitchen I see him standing on the chair while his wife sits silently at the table. I want to stop that image, keep it from moving toward an ending that continues to haunt me, preserve it in that instant before Herr Weiler kicks over the chair, that instant when Frau Weiler can still accept his promises. Fixed in my mind, they have stayed like this—in that instant when everything is still possible, when luck lies suspended and wants to mold itself into a new beginning.

The Truth About the American Soldier

If anyone had told me Rolf Brocker would be the first boy I'd kiss, I would have kicked shins. Jealous of the caring his mother gave me, he taunted me whenever he could and shoved me when others weren't looking. He was taller than I, stronger, but three weeks younger. One April, when he discovered that I had locked out his mother during a rainstorm, he pulled me into an empty doorway after church and pressed me against the wall with the weight of his body. Around his neck hung a small crucifix on a silver chain.

"Just because your parents pay her to clean up after you—" His eyes were dark. Angry. "—doesn't mean you can play stupid pranks on her."

"That's not why." I played pranks on her because she believed everything. Usually she ended up laughing with me, even if she started out angry. But it didn't seem like a good idea to tell this to Rolf.

He smelled of chalk and fresh grass clippings as he leaned against me, his body flat and hard, so different from eight years before when he'd first come to our house with his mother and we'd fought, even wrestled, over toys and snacks and games. A pudgy boy with sullen eyes, he'd lost many of our fights because I was faster and, for a few years at least, bigger. Every morning when he arrived with Frau Brocker, my mother would seclude herself in the third-floor studio where she painted all day. It was the year before Rolf and I began school, but even then we seldom played well together.

"My father was killed in the war," Rolf had told me when we met, and I'd believed him until Trudi Montag had told me that Rolf was illegitimate, that his father was an American. "One of the soldiers who was stationed here the end of the war."

The rough stucco of the doorway pressed into my back. "Let me go, Rolf." I brought my hands between us, pushed them against his stomach. The lace collar of my Sunday dress cut into my neck.

"Promise you'll leave my mother alone?"

I'd never noticed the downy hairs that grew along his chin and cheeks. His ears lay close to the sides of his head. Suddenly my face felt hot. I tried to duck out from under his arm.

He caught my wrist.

"I promise," I shouted, running from him.

But the following week Renate and I staged the worst prank yet on Rolf's mother. We set up two chairs with a wide gap between them, and when we covered them with my plaid blanket, it looked as if we had three chairs instead. Below the gap we set a water-filled tin tub from our basement.

After we cut out a crown from stiff silver paper, Renate and I sat on the two chairs, the blanket taut between us.

"Frau Brocker," I yelled, "can you help us with our play?"

When she came into my room, her face looked flushed. She'd been in the kitchen, boiling handkerchiefs and underwear. Though we had a washing machine in the cellar, she did the white laundry on the stove, insisting it wouldn't get clean otherwise. "What is it?" she asked.

"A play we have to practice," I said. "You are the princess."

"And we're the ministers of the kingdom." Renate shifted her wad of chewing gum to the inside of her other cheek.

"The old king has died"—I slowly raised the crown—"and it is our privilege to tell you that you have been chosen as his successor to the throne."

"What do I do now?" Frau Brocker's plucked eyebrows were penciled in brown. She wiped her palms on the front of her yellow dress.

"We, the ministers of the kingdom," Renate said, "would like you to accept his crown and wear it with grace. Please" —she motioned to the blanket between us—"be seated on the throne."

With both hands Frau Brocker lowered the silver crown onto her hair. "Right here, between you two?"

"Right here." Lightly, I patted the blanket next to me.

She smiled and took a step forward.

I tried not to look at Renate whose chin was trembling. "The old king would want it this way," I said in my most dignified voice.

The instant Frau Brocker sat down, Renate and I leapt up. The blanket around her back, she dropped into the tub of water. Her dress slipped up to the top of her nylons, exposing salmon-colored garters and slender thighs. Renate and I screeched with laughter. I felt it warm and low in my stomach, and rocked myself back and forth.

Renate danced around, one hand pressed against the

front of her skirt. "I'm going to pee in my pants," she gasped. "I will . . . I swear."

But Frau Brocker didn't laugh with us. The startled look on her face changed to pain.

All at once I felt sick at what I'd done to her. "Let me help you up—please?" I held out my hands.

She let out a moan. "I don't think I can."

Her buttocks were wedged in the small tin tub I'd been bathed in as an infant, and it took Renate and me several minutes to pull her out. Water had seeped through the cotton of her yellow dress, turning it darker, heavier. I felt the weight of her humiliation as she stood there in her wet dress. She didn't even look angry. Just tired. And so pale that her lipstick was like ink.

It didn't take Rolf long to find me. The next morning, when I passed the brook at the end of Schreberstrasse on my way to school, he stepped from behind a tree and blocked my path without saying a word. His dark brown hair fell over his eyebrows.

I wanted to tell him how awful I felt about hurting his mother, but I knew he wouldn't believe me. He'd only think I was a coward. "I'm not afraid of you," I said.

He squinted at me and crossed his arms in front of his windbreaker.

"What do you want?" I hooked my thumbs through the straps of my knapsack.

"I told you to leave her alone." One of his hands shot forward and grabbed my elbow. "Didn't I?"

"Get away from me, you—"

"And you promised, right?" His fingers dug into my funny bone.

I cried out.

"I guess Hanna Malter's promise doesn't mean a damn

thing." Still holding onto my elbow, he dragged me toward the brook.

As I fought to escape his grip, my shoes slipped along the muddy slope. "If you get me wet—"

That's when he pushed me. I tumbled into the icy brook. My knapsack fell forward over my head, pulling my face underwater. When I raised myself on my hands and knees, my hair hung in cold strands across my cheeks. I spit out the fishy-tasting water, pressed down my plaid skirt as it ballooned around me.

Rolf stood at a safe distance, too far to splash. "How does it feel?" His hands in the pockets of his jacket, he squinted at me.

I started shaking—from cold and shame and fear of what I was about to say—and kept shaking as I shouted at him, "At least I know who my father is! At least I'm not an illegitimate bastard like you!"

He ran and kept running until he reached the Rhein, which still flowed high from the last flood. The fine mist that rose from the river coated his face and seeped between the collar of his jacket and his skin. *Illegitimate.* When he'd heard the word, it had taken him a moment to absorb it. Another moment to doubt it. But then he knew. Knew forever. And beyond. As though the knowledge had always been with him. He felt certain everyone in Burgdorf knew. He remembered his mother's uneasiness when he'd asked her about his father, what he'd been like, and her reluctance to speak of him at all. Then the story about the fire in the kitchen—lies—all of them. Lies.

An Esso container ship made its way upstream, spitting foamy streaks of water from its back. Some of the freighters had cars parked on top. Most of them flew the German flag.

"Your father was killed in the war soon after you were born," his mother had told him when he was four. "He was a soldier."

When he'd begun asking questions, that answer was enough, but soon he wanted to know more. "Why don't we have any pictures of him?"

"They—they burned. We had a fire in the kitchen right after you were born."

Rolf stopped next to a huge willow that spread into five powerful arms where the trunk thickened above ground. Some of them were so long they hung into the river. He climbed into the dip formed by the branches of the tree. Above him, the many new leaves made a lacy pattern filled in by gray slivers of sky.

"But what did my father look like?" he had asked his mother.

"His hair was lighter than yours. He was tall and his eyes were—it's been such a long time, Rolf."

Finally she told him that his father's name was Walter. Rolf liked the name: *Walter*. It had a clear, strong sound like water rushing over rocks. Once he'd found an old photo at the bottom of her jewelry box. It showed a man whose age was hard to tell because a web of creases ran across his face and body. Taken against a light background with the sun shining, the photo was altogether too faded to make out the man's features. It looked as though a thin layer of light had wrapped itself around him and, for an instant—not more than one beat of his pulse—Rolf knew he was seeing his father.

In the mirror he sometimes stared at his dark eyes, at the wide features that resembled his mother's, and he was seized by a longing for his father that stayed with him for days before it lifted, a cold weight deep inside that could return at any moment.

At times he imagined his father tall with reddish hair, a

low voice, and kind eyes. Almost like Hanna's father who'd taught him to play chess when he was seven. With hands that were gentle even when they drilled his teeth. Some days Rolf came by Hanna's house to pick up his mother after work, but his real reason was to see Hanna's father, who usually stopped what he was doing and talked with him.

"My father was killed in the war," Rolf had told him during one of their talks and, after a brief instant, Herr Malter had nodded. "I'm sorry, Rolf." Then he'd taken his wooden chessboard from the carved chest in the living room. "Would you like to stay for a game?"

"My father was killed in the war," Rolf had told Hanna and the other kids, even the teachers, for all those years. Many of the children in Burgdorf had lost their fathers in the war, but they were all older than he. In 1946, when he was born, the war had been over for a year.

"Your father was killed in the war soon after you were born. . . . " Just a few hours earlier he'd still believed her.

Crouched in the heart of the willow, Rolf shivered. His stomach ached, and he pressed both hands against it. In a couple of months raspberries and red currants would grow along the Rhein. Below him lay pebbles in shades of brown and gray and white, some of them half buried in the sand. He would have liked to fling them at Hanna. She had everything—her own room with books and toys, two parents, even his mother, who always picked up after her.

Around the middle of the afternoon the sun appeared briefly in the sky, and when it vanished, it sucked into itself most of the light that had streaked the Rhein, replacing it with a somber gray that settled low among the boulders and shrubs, blotting out their shapes.

. . .

They began the search for Rolf late that evening—after his mother had found out he hadn't been in school, after his friends had been asked if they'd seen him.

Nobody questioned me.

When I'd returned wet and cold that morning, my teeth chattering, I'd told Frau Brocker that I'd slipped and fallen into the brook. "I'm sorry," I said to her. "I really am." And I was. But she acted as if I were talking about getting my clothes wet and made me take a hot bath, wear my flannel pajamas, and stay in bed all day with a hot-water bottle at my feet.

My parents were among dozens of adults who searched for Rolf while I lay awake, waiting for their return. It was silent in our apartment, silent and too hot. I imagined Rolf somewhere alone with his pain. My face burned, but my hands felt like ice. I threw off my covers. From the drawer in my night table I took out the blue journal Veronika had given me.

My parents had taken my flashlight as well as the large one from the kitchen. I pictured a file of flickering light beams in the woods near the abandoned flour mill and among the piles of debris at the dump, along the river and around the quarry hole. I imagined their voices calling his name—short sounds swallowed by the darkness. What if Rolf lay somewhere with a broken leg or, worse yet, what if he were dead?

He had to be all right. He had to be. But what would he say when they found him? Suddenly I was afraid of him. Everyone would be angry at me, especially my parents. Frau Brocker would quit her job. Herr Pastor Beier would assign me hours of prayer. I wrote in my journal about what I had done to Rolf. If only I could find him first. If only I could talk to my parents about what I had said. But with each hour they stayed out, my crime seemed to grow, and by the time they came back at daybreak, cold and tired, it was impossible to tell them.

Frau Brocker did not come in that morning. When I got dressed, my parents were sleeping. I packed my knapsack for school but hid it behind the lilac bush in our backyard. The least I could do was search for Rolf. If my parents found out I'd skipped classes, it was nothing compared to what I'd already done.

Rolf woke to the sound of waves slapping against the jetties, and in that blurred moment of emerging from sleep, he was six again and the water was slapping against the side of his house while he knelt on a chair, looking from the fourth-floor window into the street where people were floating in rowboats and kayaks.

He blinked. That had happened the year the dike in Burgdorf had broken. The Rhein had frozen, blocking the flow of water, and when the ice melted, masses of water pressed forward until the river left the bed where it belonged. It flooded the meadows and raged against the dike which people tried to support with sand-filled burlap bags and slabs of sod. But the river forced a gap into the barricade and icy water rushed through, widening the break; it washed across streets, spilled down basement steps, and climbed up table legs on all first floors.

People moved their belongings to the upper stories of their houses. Rolf helped Herr Flemern, who lived downstairs, up the steps, guiding the old man's skinny elbow as he wheezed and stopped on each landing. Rolf's mother took in the retired tailor although their apartment had only one bedroom, which she shared with Rolf's grandmother. She let the old man sleep on the living room sofa—Rolf's bed—and pushed together two overstuffed chairs in front of the window as a sleeping area for Rolf.

For five days and nights long threads of rain linked the sky to the surface of the gray water, which rose steadily. In St. Martin's Church the water covered the pews, and

Herr Pastor Beier held mass at the chapel which stood on a hill far from the dike.

That Sunday Hanna's father picked up Rolf and his mother in a rowboat to take them to the chapel. He smiled at Rolf as he lifted him into the boat. Sitting on the dentist's knees, Rolf helped move the oars through the sluggish water. If his father were alive, he'd row the boat with him just like this. Hanna's father tied the boat to a maple at the bottom of the hill where other boats were already fastened to trees and fences. He held Rolf's hand as they walked in their Sunday clothes up the path toward the white chapel, but when Rolf saw that Hanna and her mother were already waiting, he pulled his hand away. More pigeons than he'd ever seen sat on the bell tower and slate roof; they screeched from the crowns of the poplars and swarmed low above the waters that covered the surrounding wheat fields.

The flood drenched the cemetery and toppled several headstones; it uprooted many of the shrubs that adorned the graves and left long indentations in the earth as if some of the coffins had been stolen.

As the slapping of waves against the jetties blended with the sounds that Rolf remembered from the flood, his eyes closed. He felt drowsy, heavy, and just before he sagged into sleep, he recalled seeing straw in the upper branches of some trees after the gray waters had receded.

When I found him half hidden by the leaves of the willow, he was lying on his side, knees drawn up to his chest. Even in his sleep he shivered. His face looked pale and damp, and as I tried to think of a way to wake him without startling him, he opened his eyes and stared at me without moving. His eyes were three different shades of brown, lightest around the pupils, then darkening and ending in a deep brown ring where the white started. All at once I felt I didn't know him at all—my enemy for years—and because I didn't know him, I could say anything. Or nothing. I stared back at him.

"What do you want?" His voice made me jump.

I touched his sleeve. Pulled back my hand. "They've been searching for you all night."

"Go away." He sat up. Hunched his shoulders as if to hide himself in the hollow formed by his body.

I took a long breath, then another. "I—I was rotten. I shouldn't have said—"

"Who told you about him?" The right side of his face was red and puckered where the bark had pressed into it.

"Trudi Montag."

He groaned. "That means everyone knows."

Two ducks bobbed around the submerged trunk of a willow. A brisk wind moved the smaller branches. I rubbed my arms.

"I hate her," he said, "for not telling me. For having me." He rested his head on his knees. His voice sounded hoarse. "What else do you know about him?"

"That he is an American."

"What?"

"He was stationed in Burgdorf for a while—in the house where you live." I looked away from him. The sand was dark and wet above the water line. "I guess that's when they—your mother and he—you know . . . "

"What else?"

A freighter passed by, raising waves that broke against the embankment.

"Hanna—what else?" Even then he was good at persisting with questions which pushed you into answers you didn't want to give. It was a skill he would develop further in law school and court, a skill which would earn him a certain admiration from the people in Burgdorf where he would choose to set up his practice fifteen years later.

"Hanna—"

I twisted my left foot from side to side, worked it

through the top layer of pebbles and sand. "He was married."

He started to cry then—long, raging sobs that made me want to bolt. I climbed into the willow next to him. He smelled like my wool coat after it got drenched in the rain. Cautiously I laid one hand on his shoulder and when he didn't pull away, I rubbed back and forth across the trembling I felt through his windbreaker.

"Did he have other kids?"

"I don't know."

He wiped one sleeve across his face. Sniffled, "Then find out."

"You could ask your mother."

"No," he said. "No."

"Or my parents."

He shook his head. "Ask Trudi Montag," he said. "And then come back here."

"Here? It's cold. Besides—everyone's worried about you. They've been searching for you all night."

"Who?"

"My parents. Matthias Berger. The Talmeisters. Frau Weiler. Lots of people. Your mother . . . "

"If you tell her where I am—"

"I won't tell anyone."

"How do I know?"

That's when I did it—pressed my lips against his, so hard I could feel his teeth beneath the softness. He sat very still, and I didn't pull away. Eyes open, we stared at each other. His lips were dry, his mouth larger than mine. It seemed like a long time since I'd been afraid of him.

"How—" I swallowed and moved my head back. "How about after I find out more—will you come back with me then?"

He nodded. With one thumb he pushed a strand of hair from my face. "I think so," he said.

. . .

Before I left, I promised him once more I wouldn't tell anyone where he was hiding. It was a promise I kept despite the conviction that what I was doing was getting worse. If Rolf disappeared from the willow and never returned—I tried not to imagine him running along the river in the direction of Düsseldorf or floating away on one of the barges.

When I opened the door to Trudi Montag's pay-library, she didn't even ask me why I wasn't in school. So filled was she with speculations about Rolf's disappearance, that I only had to prod her lightly.

"Maybe Rolf went to live with his father," I suggested.

"Don't be silly, Hanna. That man's clear cross the ocean. In one of those skyscrapers. I think Rolf just got tired taking care of his grandmother. Living in that cramped apartment isn't—"

I tried the name of the American city that sounded most familiar. "In New York?"

She looked up. Frowned. "No, Florida. Where they grow oranges in their backyards." Since Trudi Montag had relatives in America, she considered herself the local authority on that country.

"Which city in Florida?"

"Let me think. . . . Wait—something with an M or a P."

"Did he have other children?"

"Who knows?" Trudi Montag shrugged. "Some of the soldiers showed us pictures of their wives and kids. This one had a wife for sure. A model, he told me when he first came to town." She described him to me as a tall man with blond hair and a small birthmark on one temple, but she didn't remember the color of his eyes. "He liked to dance," she said. "Both of them—Klara Brocker too. He'd rest his chin on top of her head—that's how much taller he was."

On my way back I stopped at Becker's grocery store next door and bought two chocolate bars with hazelnuts for Rolf. He moved aside to let me climb into the heart of the willow with him, and while I told him what Trudi Montag had said, he ate the chocolate, chewing slowly the way he always did, even though he hadn't eaten since the day before.

"Most models don't want kids," I said. "It ruins their figures."

"How would you know?"

"Things I read . . . They don't want to stretch their stomachs. So maybe you're his only child. Maybe—are you going to look for him?"

He crumpled the silver foil into tight balls. "You go home now."

"What about you?"

"In a while."

"What if you change your mind?"

"I won't."

But I was afraid he might vanish again. I kept urging him to go first and was surprised when he finally agreed. As he crossed the meadow, he glanced back toward the willow and raised one hand. Then he climbed the dike.

The truth about the American Soldier became our secret, a secret that became as strong a bond between us as the kisses we exchanged. It was strange, Rolf said, to know his father might still be alive. But he didn't have any idea how to go about finding him.

Though he told me about the photo in his mother's jewelry box, I didn't see it until one afternoon that August when Rolf and I climbed the four flights of shadowy stairs to his apartment on Barbarossastrasse 15. He'd just had his hair cut; except for a pale stripe of skin along his ears and neck, he was tanned a smooth brown, and the sun had bleached the fine hairs on his cheeks.

His grandmother was asleep in the room she shared with Rolf's mother, her frail body covered by a worn night-gown. A feather comforter lay on the floor next to her bed. The right side of her face was pulled down toward her slack jaw from a stroke that had left the right side of her body paralyzed. Eleven times so far it had seemed as though she were ready to die, and Frau Brocker had sent Rolf to fetch the increasingly reluctant Herr Pastor Beier who knew, along with the whole town, that whenever he administered last rites to the old woman, she recovered within a few days as if cured by his final absolution.

A blue pack of Gauloises lay on the windowsill. On the table stood a teapot, a cup, and an empty plate. Every noon Frau Brocker carried over some of the food she had cooked at our house, sat on the edge of her mother's bed, and fed her with a spoon.

"Stay here," Rolf whispered.

From the door frame I watched him walk toward his grandmother, pick up the comforter, and spread it gently across her. At the foot end of his mother's bed he crouched and slipped a flat red leather box from under her mattress. He walked past me on tiptoes and I followed him into the kitchen, which smelled of medicine and bleached laundry. We sat at the table and Rolf smoothed out the linen table-cloth before he opened the box.

"Here." He took a creased photo from beneath the glossy jumble of fake pearls, ornate pins, and rings with glass stones.

I held the picture in both hands. It felt soft, as if it had been touched many times. The man in the photo wore trousers with a belt and a white shirt. He had a narrow face, and his eyebrows were a darker shade of blond than his hair. Rolf leaned forward, looking at the man's faded features with such longing that I imagined his father reaching up toward the branches of an orange tree under a sun that was bright, white, a sun that soaked its rays into his shirt as he stood in that one luminous moment before breaking off an orange, forever reaching, forever there.

✍ Saving a Life

The summer of 1960 I was fourteen and I wanted to save someone's life. It was the only thing I was sure I could do. About everything else I felt uncertain: my legs were too long, my face was too round, my hair was too straight. . . . Although the woman who wanted to marry my father—Fräulein Mahler—told me I was beautiful, I knew she only said it so I wouldn't try to talk my father out of marrying her. She'd inherited the Mahler department store in Düsseldorf, and whenever she visited us, she gave me books or records or white chocolates in silver foil. When she smiled, I could see the gold crowns my father had put on her back teeth. She was older than my father's other female patients who'd brought cakes and casseroles to our house after my mother had died in April.

My mother had been a good swimmer. I had that from her. I'd passed each test with the highest marks, including the life-saving test and had dreams of proving myself as a saver of lives. It would be better if the drowning person were a man twice my weight. *He struggles. He's heavy and balding like Herr Stosick, who plays chess with my father on Monday nights, and I stun him by knocking my fist against his temple. Keeping his chin above water with one arm, I drag him to safety. Sometimes it takes over an hour to get him to shore while people watch from the dike and admire my courage. Other times I save him in less than ten minutes. During the TV interview I speak firmly and smile without showing my gums. In front of the bathroom mirror I practice different versions of that dazzling, yet modest smile I'll flash when the mayor hands me the medal. I make sure they film me in my new swimsuit.*

But the people who swam in the Rhein were cautious and stayed close to the pebbled embankment. Adults waded in up to their waists, and children held on to inner tubes. Here, the river was wide and flowed evenly; it ran straight without obstructions, and the next bend was half a kilometer downstream. Along the river stretched the town of Burgdorf, both ends clinging to its bank like tentacles that thinned out against the boundaries of adjoining towns.

Whenever the sun became so hot that it made me dizzy, I left my watching post on the flat boulders at the end of the jetty and swam out into the river; floating on my back without moving my arms or legs, I let the current carry me. Sometimes I pretended my mother was next to me: the slapping of the waves became the sound of her arms parting the water. But then I'd remember the car accident and feel everything happen all over again: the call from the police; rushing with my father to the hospital; arriving too late. It was one of the few times I'd seen my father cry. In the corridor of the hospital he'd gathered me into his arms, my damp face pressed against his jacket. His arms and shoulders trembled as he cried with me until my terror became contained within his sorrow.

He said the river was too dangerous. He asked me not to swim there. Just as he had asked my mother not to smoke or drive so fast. Renate and Rolf swam in the town pool; they said the Rhein was too dirty. I found it boring to paddle in water that didn't carry me forward; yet, I could never stay in the river as long as I wanted because it was impossible to swim against the current, which ran at eight kilometers an hour. Whatever distance I drifted, I had to walk back. Frau Brocker knew I swam in the Rhein, but she was good at keeping secrets. She had never told my father about all the times my mother and I used to swim while it rained. On summer days when dark clouds moved across the sky, my mother would clean the paint from her hands and leave her studio; we'd pull on our swimsuits and loose dresses over them, then head for the river or the quarry.

My mother swam with smooth strokes. She didn't like wearing a bathing camp. Her blond hair looked darker when it was wet, straighter, and it trailed behind her. When I grew confident swimming in the quarry, she took me to the river, where we rode the current together. I let my ball with the sisal net keep me above water. By the time I was seven, I didn't need it any longer.

One Sunday afternoon, only a year ago, we'd floated for hours, talking and laughing; sometimes we were silent and let the sun warm our faces. It was the kind of silence that fills you with light and makes you believe you can do anything you want. We drifted until we got to my father's favorite restaurant, the Kaisershafen Gasthaus, which overlooked the Rhein. High above us, in the turrets, the many small windows glistened like mirrors. Every November we had my father's family reunion here: uncles in expensive suits with vests; aunts who wore silk dresses in dark colors; cousins who went to private schools and talked about dances and tennis matches; Great-aunt Augusta with her opal ring and varicose veins; Great-uncle Viktor with his cane that was covered with silver emblems of places he'd never been to.

Except for Oma, none of the relatives liked my mother. I'm not sure why—perhaps because she wore bright colors and had gone to art school. She was taller than the other women; yet, during those reunions she felt small to me, and I stayed near her. She smoked more than usual, inhaling quickly, lighting a new cigarette as soon as the last one was finished.

That summer afternoon my mother and I—wearing our wet swimsuits—climbed the stone steps that led to the terrace of the Kaisershafen Gasthaus. She smiled as we walked past the planters that overflowed with fuchsias, past the tables with their striped umbrellas, where people sat in their Sunday clothes, eating pastries and drinking coffee or lemonade. Everyone watched us. My mother's back was straight, and her hair lay like a silk scarf on her shoulders, covering most of the freckles that spread across her back. Through the double glass doors we walked into the lobby where she asked the head waiter for the phone so she could call my father to pick us up. We left dark puddles on the carpet and on the upholstery of our car. My father's face looked pale and helpless as he drove us home. "What you're doing is dangerous," he told both of us.

The second Wednesday of August Fräulein Mahler came to our house and invited me to go shopping with her. "So we can get to know each other better," she said.

I wished I could find real reasons to dislike her, reasons that would convince my father to stop seeing her, but all I could think was that she was too friendly and kept giving me things. "I've already made plans," I said. "With friends."

For a moment she seemed disappointed, though I was sure it was only an act for my father's benefit. She was about my father's age, nearly twenty years older than my mother, and I couldn't imagine her ever doing anything dangerous.

It was his day off, and he sat close to her on the sofa in our living room, taking small bites from a buttered slice of raisin bread she had baked for us. His cardigan was unbuttoned, and he still wore his deerskin slippers. On the wall across from him hung my mother's painting of the flooded meadow between the Rhein and the dike, the dark reflections of willows blurred in the silver-green waters.

"Can't you change your plans, Hanna?" my father asked softly. New strands of gray wove through his reddish-brown beard, and the bald spot on top of his head had widened.

I wanted to shout that my mother had been dead less than four months, wanted him to remember her as he sat there so snug next to Fräulein Mahler with her turquoise dress and her gold teeth, but somehow—that moment—I couldn't even remember my mother's face.

Fräulein Mahler smiled at him. "Hanna and I will have many other times together." She waved aside the flies that had come in through the open window, wrapped two pieces of her raisin bread in a napkin, and handed them to me. "In case you get hungry." Her fingernails were perfect ovals the color of squashed cherries.

I said, "Thank you," as always when she forced her presents on me, presents I never used. Well—never wasn't quite true. I'd eaten some of her white chocolates, though I hadn't enjoyed them, and I'd read two of her books before stacking them behind the hamper in back of my closet with her other stuff.

When Fräulein Mahler had started coming to our house, Frau Brocker and I had thought up several plots to get rid of her, from chasing her out the door with a broom to questioning her sanity by pretending we'd never seen her before; but then our housekeeper had begun to like her. "She's good for your father, Hanna."

As I pushed my bicycle out of the shed in our backyard, one of the dried blossoms from the lilac bush scratched against my forehead. Though the leaves had stayed green, the blossoms had shriveled into brown scepters. I ripped one of them off the bush and crumbled it between my fingers; it looked like tobacco but felt like dry dirt. The day of my mother's funeral the blossoms had been white and I'd dropped a bunch of the lilacs into her open grave.

Trudi Montag stood in front of the house across the street, talking with Frau Talmeister, who leaned out of her window, a cup of coffee in her hand. The sidewalk was a slippery mess with all the cherries that had fallen from the Talmeisters' tree. Despite the heat, Trudi Montag wore a pink cardigan over her housedress, and her O-shaped legs were in ankle socks. Since my mother's death I hadn't wanted to be with any of my friends, not even with Trudi Montag in her pay-library.

Both women waved to me; I raised one hand, though I would have liked to pretend I hadn't seen them. They were probably talking about my father and Fräulein Mahler, whose BMW was parked in our driveway entirely too often.

At the end of the street, the Hansen bakery truck pulled away from the curb, and I pushed back against my bike pedals to slow down. Manfred Weiler's mother walked toward me carrying two loaves of *Schwarzbrot*, looking down as if counting the cracks in the sidewalk. In the years since her husband had hung himself, she hadn't come to our door, though she still lived in our building. Her son, Manfred, dropped off the rent check on the first of each month. He'd become one of those boys who stood in groups at street corners, watching girls' legs and whistling dirty. When we were six, we had dared each other to steal an egg from his father's chicken coop. With a sharp stone we'd jabbed a hole into the shell and taken turns sucking it out, lying to each other about how delicious it was.

I rode my bike to the Rhein and dropped it next to the boulder I used as a lookout. The air was hazy and tinged with the scent of grass and wildflowers—bright red poppies and blue cornflowers—that grew in the meadow between the dike and the river. Streaks of sunlight broke the

white-crested waves into layers the color of slate. I ripped
Fräulein Mahler's raisin bread into shreds and tossed them
into the water, satisfied at the thought of fat gray fish
crowding below and feeding on them.

The river was calmer than during the spring when I
sometimes came here to watch the floods that swirled
against the dike, covering the lower trunks of the trees,
making them look less sturdy than on land. The worst flood
my mother had ever seen had happened when she was a
girl: the Rhein had flooded nearly a hundred towns, killing
five people, eighteen cows, and seven horses in Burgdorf
alone. It had torn out trees and created a deep basin near
the embankment; after the floods had receded, the basin
remained filled with water and became a swimming hole.

When I was smaller, I used to ride my sled down the
dike in the winter; my mother would run alongside, laughing, catching me whenever I fell off, and then pull the sled
with me on it back up the dike. Her hair would be tangled,
her face red from the wind.

My stomach felt withered and cold. Clasping my arms
around my knees, I held my legs close and rocked myself
back and forth. From the river sounded the blast of a
freighter's whistle, deep and sorrowful like the bellows of
the cattle that often drifted from the Braunmeiers' farm
when dusk set in.

A flat-nosed barge pulled its heavy load upstream. Long
and narrow, it had two cabins, one in front and one in
back. They were painted white, their roofs and smoke-
stacks red. Between them stretched a clothesline with laundry that whipped the wind like an exhibit of odd flags: a
child's yellow dress, white bedsheets, a blue towel.

I wished I could live on one of those barges with the river
people. Float far away and never come back. I scratched
my shoulders where the last sunburn had peeled, leaving
shiny patches of new skin. At the river's edge, next to the
weathered bench, two women had spread a blanket. One

of them held a baby whom she nursed by covering her breasts with a towel and holding the baby's head beneath. The other woman had a small son who tottered around on unsteady legs, tore clumps of camomile from the meadow, and presented them to his mother, their dirty roots swinging against his chest.

Yesterday I had walked upriver for almost three kilometers, way past the meadow where the architect Siegfried Tegern used to take his seven dogs. I'd let the current carry me back to where I'd started. But today I didn't feel like walking. I picked at the blue nubs of nylon on my old bathing suit, pulling until they hung by one last transparent thread.

In the middle of the Rhein, two barges strained upstream, connected by a long cable. Puffs of steam blew from the stack of the first barge. Where the smoke came out, it looked smudged, but the wind blew it toward the sky, fraying it until it became white and, further up, almost translucent. I could see where the steel cable from the stern of the first freighter entered the water and where it came out again, fastened to the bow of the second ship. I imagined myself swimming out there, holding on to the cable, and letting the barges pull me upriver. I'd get a closer glimpse of the people who lived on them. As long as I stayed away from the hulls, the suction around them couldn't pull me under. Then I'd be able to drift back here without having to walk.

Waves splashed around me as I swam out to where the barges approached. The swift water felt good against my body. I felt strong. Nothing could happen to me. Floating in the current with me, my mother had told me about whirlpools and what I should do if I got caught in one. She told me of people who'd drowned fighting the downward spiral, trying to break out of its sides—something that was impossible. The only way to survive a whirlpool, she said, was to go down with it as deeply as possible and then,

where it weakened at the bottom, swim out. I knew I could
even save someone caught in a whirlpool.

I waited for the freighters at a safe distance, treading
water with my legs. After the stern of the first barge passed
me, I swam out to find a good spot where I could grasp the
cable. I reached for it about one meter before it dipped
underwater.

The pain was incredible as the skin was torn off my
palms. It felt as if the force of the barges straining against
the river would tear out my arms. My hands slipped to
where the fraying cable disappeared in the current, and I
was thrust beneath it. I fought to get away, but the cable
cut across my stomach and pulled my head underwater.
Somewhere I'd heard your entire life flashes in front of you
before you die. Oddly calm, I found myself waiting for
that moment, one compact time capsule. But all I felt was
a dark pressure against my ears, my mouth, a pressure that
would surely fill me, soothe me, replace me if I let it. For
an instant I considered giving in—it would be so easy—
but then I thought of my mother on that empty stretch of
highway, driving too fast, too close to the concrete divider.
Something within me protested, and I fought once more
against the cable.

But it only cut deeper into my stomach, my arms. My
lungs hurt as though they were about to burst. I pushed
down and away, arms and legs kicking, freeing myself from
the cable, then up, up. I stretched for air. Was blinded by
yellow dots. My eyes ached. A deep, hollow sound, then
voices, all at once, loud and angry. And the barge, the
second barge—blurred at first—was less than ten meters
from me, advancing. Aboard two men and a woman
shouted. Waved me away.

As fast as I could, I swam toward the embankment and
pulled myself out of the river. I crawled on my hands and
knees, fell onto the hard pebbles. My hands were bleeding,
palms raw with steel splinters, blackened by tar. My bath-

ing suit was ripped. Bleeding welts had sprung up on my thighs and stomach.

It took months for the skin on my body to heal, and for the splinters, which the doctor could not remove, to work their way to the surface of my palms.

In the evenings my father spread ointment on my hands, and I tried not to flinch at its cold sting. "If only you didn't have to take such risks. . . ," he'd say as he wrapped fresh lengths of gauze around my outstretched hands. It sounded as if he were talking to my mother.

I was still picking at those splinters in November when my father took Fräulein Mahler to the family reunion at the Kaisershafen Gasthaus. She wore a brown silk dress and smiled with her expensive teeth as she admired my great-aunt Augusta's opal ring. Uncle Viktor showed her the silver Venice emblem on his cane, and Aunt Bettina invited her to visit for a weekend in Köln. My father looked so pleased that I couldn't bear to watch.

I walked out through the double glass doors and onto the empty terrace. Tables and umbrellas had been stored away for the winter. The huge planters were empty, the wide stone steps covered with a delicate pattern of frost. Already the light was changing to a hazy shade of gray, and in the turrets above me most of the small windows were lit. One hand on the iron railing, I walked down the stairs to where the smoke-colored waves tossed themselves against the embankment. I sat on a step, and as I traced the swirls of frost with one finger, I had a sudden image of my mother, climbing the stairs in the red swimsuit she'd lost in the North Sea, smiling to herself as she walked into the lobby, past the bewildered head waiter, and flung open the door to the dining room where the relatives were gathered.

My father and Fräulein Mahler married the following February, less than a year after my mother's accident. By then I was in boarding school—a request I'd made which my father had approved after much hesitation. Fräulein Mahler had surprised me by trying to talk me into living at home with her and my father. When he picked me up from school the day before the wedding, he drove silently, and I figured he was worried about how I might behave during the ceremony, but then I realized it was something else when he reached over to me and said, "It doesn't mean that I'll ever forget her." His hand felt warm and light on my arm.

In St. Martin's Church I knelt between Renate and Rolf in the first of the birch pews. A red carpet partially covered the marble steps that led to the altar where Herr Pastor Beier stood one level above my father and Fräulein Mahler. The three stained-glass windows behind the marble altar filtered the winter light through their intricate pattern of red, white, and black crosses.

As my father exchanged vows with Fräulein Mahler, I reached for a black prayer book and held it closed in my hands. Against the smooth leather binding, I felt the scars on my palms. Perhaps I needed to believe in something that day, something just for myself, because I emerged from the church convinced that the scars on my hands would guard me like magic against making mistakes in the future. But of course it didn't work that way, and it only occurred to me much later that the summer I was fourteen I had saved a life—not the life of a stranger as I had imagined—but the life I had taken for granted and which, in the years to come, I would take for granted again.